The Glow of the Spotlight

My Journey with Rebecca

by Jacqueline Dembar Greene

★ AmericanGirl®

D1020465

Published by American Girl Publishing
Copyright © 2014 American Girl

Questions or comments? Call 1-800-845-0005,
visit **americangirl.com**, or write to Customer Service,
American Girl, 8400 Fairway Place, Middleton, WI 53562.

Printed in China
14 15 16 17 18 19 20 LEO 10 9 8 7 6 5 4 3 2 1

With much gratitude to Erin Falligant

Cover image by Michael Dwornik and Juliana Kolesova
Russian doll charm by Bohème Jewelry

Cataloging-in-Publication Data available from the Library of Congress

To Elly,
for friendship that travels through all times

Beforever

Beforever is about making connections.
It's about exploring the past, finding your
place in the present, and thinking about the
possibilities your future can bring. And it's about
seeing the common thread that ties girls from
all times together. The inspiring characters you
will meet stand up for what they care about
most: Helping others. Protecting the earth.
Overcoming injustice. Through their courageous
stories, discover how staying true to your own
beliefs will help make your world better
today—and tomorrow.

was just jealous. As soon as I said it, I felt a terrible hole in my chest. I apologized right away, but Liz threw her tap shoes into her bag and stormed out of the dressing room.

I don't want to lose a good friend over a dance recital, but I just don't know what to do now.

The store is so quiet I can hear the clock ticking, and it's hard to concentrate. Unlike Megan, who's a whiz at math, I've never been very good at it. Why do I need to memorize the times tables when I'm going to be a famous dancer?

Turn to page 6.

Every time I look at the times tables, the numbers dance all over the page instead of lining up in my head. I glance up at the grandfather clock ticking in a corner of the antique shop. If it's showing the right time, it's 5:41.

I try again. "Mom, we're going to miss the ferry." We live in New Jersey, which is across the Hudson River from New York. We ride the ferry into the city every week for my dance classes.

Mom gives me a sympathetic smile. "It'll just be a few more minutes, honey. We've got plenty of time." She hands Megan her phone. "Give your father a call and let him know we'll be home in time to make dinner."

I close the workbook and rummage through my purse, finding two quarters and a crumpled dollar bill. Maybe there's something interesting here that doesn't cost too much. I wander over to a table filled with old-fashioned toy cars, metal mechanical banks, and china dolls. Suddenly I spot a painted wooden doll. It has a flat bottom and stands there looking at me sweetly. Swirly designs with leaves and flowers surround a smiling face. Painted hands are folded across a flowery dress. As I reach for it, the dealer says, "That's an old

Russian nesting doll." I guess I look clueless, because
she explains, "If you pull the top and bottom apart,
there are smaller dolls nesting inside."

I tug the two halves, and sure enough, a smaller
doll appears inside. Cute! On I go, opening each doll to
reveal a smaller one. The last one is so tiny I can't imagine how the artist painted it so perfectly. I line up the
dolls on the table, falling in love with each one. I turn
over the largest doll, looking for a price tag.

The dealer studies me with a curious expression. "I
played with those often as a girl. I'm rather attached to
them," she says. "Do put the set back together for me,
won't you?" She turns back to my mother.

I don't see a price tag, but if the set is special to her,
I suppose it must be expensive. I sit down on the floor
and begin putting the dolls back together. I place the
tiniest one inside the next smallest doll, carefully lining
up the painted hands, when the room starts to spin.
I steady myself against the table, thinking the audition
must have really worn me out. Then everything around
me is lost in a blur.

꧁ *Turn to page 8.*

A cool breeze washes over me and I blink. Instead of a table of antique toys beside me, I'm sitting against a low brick wall at the edge of a flat rooftop. My heart starts pounding. What happened to the antique store, and Mom, and Megan—and *where on earth am I?* Standing up, I peer over the edge of the wall to the street below. It's lined with a row of tidy three-story apartment houses that have high front steps. At least I'm still in Manhattan—I think. But instead of honking taxis and cars, the street is clogged with people and horse-drawn wagons. A horn sounds: *Ah-oo-ga! Ah-ooh-ga!* I shake my head and blink, but when I look again, a shiny black antique car comes chugging and sputtering up the street. Is this a parade?

Behind me, a soothing voice says, "There you go, Gray-Wing." Turning around, I see a girl about my age with long copper-brown hair, feeding a pigeon in a cage. In fact, there's a whole row of pigeon cages against the far wall, and I hear a chorus of coos. Could this be a dream?

Suddenly, the girl begins to sing in a beautiful clear voice. I duck behind a stack of wooden crates and watch her. She's wearing old-fashioned high-button

boots and a dress with violet stripes. Her hair is tied back with a big purple velvet ribbon. I guess she likes purple as much as I do.

If this is a dream, it sure feels real. Should I try to talk to the girl?

She's singing to the pigeons as if they're her audience, but she's nothing like some of the show-offs at the dance studio. I start to stand, but then think better of it. It's all just too strange!

I glance down and realize that I'm still holding the two smallest Russian dolls, one nestled inside the other. I flash back to my last moment in the antique store, when I put the dolls together. Did the dolls somehow, magically . . . ? It doesn't make any sense, but then dreams often don't. My fingers trembling, I separate the larger doll, so that the smallest one peeks out. Then I fit the larger doll back together, lining up the design of the hands—and once again everything around me spins into a blur and disappears.

Turn to page 10.

Almost instantly, the dizziness passes and I'm back inside the antique shop. I check the grandfather clock and am startled to see that it reads 5:41. Not a minute passed while I was gone.

Disoriented, I step away from the table and stumble into a small wooden wagon filled with dolls. There's a huge clatter as the dolls fall and knock one another over like dominoes. Mom gives me a sharp look.

"Nothing's broken!" I call, feeling shaky.

Megan slams her book closed. "Can't you stay still for one minute? I'm trying to read my science book. Did you already finish studying for your multiplication quiz?" But Megan really isn't asking, because she knows the answer is no.

I stare down at the dolls in my hand. I don't know if I fell into a dream or a hidden time warp, but whatever it was, I want go back. If I can get there again, this time I'll talk to that girl who was singing and feeding the pigeons. Maybe we could become friends. And since no time passes here while I'm in that other world, Mom won't even notice that I'm gone. She's still haggling with the dealer over the price of the mirror, but we'll have to leave soon to catch the ferry. This is my

A Journey Begins

This book is about Rebecca, but it's also about a girl like you who travels back in time to Rebecca's world of 1914. You, the reader, get to decide what happens in the story. The choices you make will lead to different journeys and new discoveries.

When you reach a page in this book that asks you to make a decision, choose carefully. The decisions you make will lead to different endings. (Hint: Use a pencil to check off your choices. That way, you'll never read the same story twice.)

Want to try another ending? Read the book again—and then again. Find out what happens to you and Rebecca when you make different choices.

Before your journey ends, take a peek into the past, on page 154, to discover more about Rebecca's time.

The dance audition is finally over, and it was definitely my best performance ever. Still, when my teacher, Ms. Amelia, chose me to do a solo for the winter recital, I was stunned. I never expected her to pick me after what happened last spring: I was onstage with my class, and when I looked out at the audience, I froze. I couldn't dance—or even move. Ms. Amelia actually had to come out and lead me off! I'll never live it down. Even my twin sister, Megan, who rarely misses a chance to embarrass me, tried to make me feel better by being extra nice for weeks. So after today's audition, I'm beyond thrilled that my teacher had enough faith to let me try again.

But as happy as I was, it didn't last long—the day ended up in a terrible fight with my friend Liz. She got totally rattled when she flubbed a few steps of her routine. She managed to finish, but definitely didn't do as well as she could have, and she didn't get a special part in the recital. I tried to make her feel better, but she accused me of thinking I'm a better dancer than she is, which isn't true at all. The truth is that the thought of dancing by myself on that huge stage makes my stomach churn. But I know that if I ever want to be a pro, I have to get over my stage fright!

Now it's late afternoon, and Mom, Megan, and I are walking down West Thirty-Ninth Street toward the pier to catch the ferry home. Suddenly my mother stops in her tracks. "Oh, look at this gorgeous antique shop," she says. "I've been wanting to stop in here for ages." She peers into the window. "And I think I see the perfect mirror. We have some time to kill before we catch the ferry. Let's take a look."

Megan and I follow Mom into the shop, rolling our eyes at each other. The mirror is just inside, and I have to admit that it's really rather elegant, with leafy vines carved into its dark wood frame. I can just picture it in her bedroom. Mom walks casually up to the dealer and asks how old it is. The dealer looks kind of like an antique herself. Her hair is pure white, and she's wearing a long skirt and a high-collared blouse with a brooch at the neck.

While Mom and the dealer discuss the price, I stand in front of the mirror, admiring the way the glass can tilt forward or back in its stand. I'm in my favorite school outfit, and I twirl in front of my reflection. The shimmery purple fabric of my skirt fans out, and the

sequined flowers on the front sparkle.

After the audition, I had wanted to wear my awesome new dance costume, which has sequined black shorts, and a black and white top with a bow tie. It's like a girl's version of a tuxedo. It would have been so cool to walk around Manhattan wearing it; people might have thought I was from a real Broadway show! But Mom reminded me that it was too chilly outside to wear it, and I definitely wouldn't want to mess it up before the recital.

I can't resist doing a bit of my dance routine while I look in the mirror. Megan groans as if I'm totally embarrassing her. As usual, she's wearing jeans and a baggy sweatshirt that says *Harvard*. As if she's going there anytime soon. I mean, we're only ten!

Megan and I are twins, but we don't look alike or do the same things. She loves museums, I love theater. She wants to be a doctor, like our dad, while I want to be a dancer. We don't even like the same books or video games. Sometimes I wish we were better friends, but most of the time it feels as if she and I are just plain opposites.

Like right now: she plops herself down in an

overstuffed armchair and pulls out her science book.

"I see Megan is getting a start on her homework," Mom says to me. "I might need a few minutes to decide about this mirror, so why don't you study your times tables. Didn't you say there's a quiz tomorrow?"

"*Mo-o-om* . . ." I protest, but she waves me off. She's already bargaining with the antique dealer, trying to get the woman to drop her asking price. She points out a few chips in the glass.

The dealer considers this, and then shakes her head.

"How about free delivery?" my mother presses.

This is going to take a while. Sighing, I plop down in a creaking leather chair and drag my dance bag closer.

Inside, next to my arithmetic workbook, are my tap shoes and the tuxedo costume. I open my book to the first page of times tables and try to concentrate on that instead of thinking about my fight with Liz.

I don't really know how the argument got started. I was trying to make Liz feel better, but she accused me of only caring because I knew I had a solo. It isn't true! I was so hurt that I lashed out and told her she

only chance to go back and meet that girl. And if I go,
I won't have to deal with Megan, or Liz, or times tables!

Once again, I pull the bigger doll apart, and then
push it together, aligning the pattern. In a flash, the
room spins, and when I open my eyes and steady
myself, I'm back on the same rooftop with the girl in the
purple dress. I take a small step forward and clear my
throat. I try not to startle her, but she jumps when she
hears me. "Sorry," I apologize, and then wonder what
to say next.

Before I can come up with an explanation of how
I got there, the girl smiles.

"You must be Daisy!" she exclaims. I have no idea
who Daisy is, but I have no time to tell her who I really
am before she rattles on. "Cousin Max told Papa you
might be coming to stay with us for a few days. It must
be so exciting to be on the vaudeville circuit."

Did she say *vaudeville*? The theme of the winter
recital (when I'll be dancing a solo!) is based on old
vaudeville shows. We'll be dancing to songs that were
popular a hundred years ago. My tap class is doing a
dance that Ms. Amelia says was a big hit back then.
Of course, this girl couldn't possibly know about that.

But she seems to think vaudeville is cool, so maybe
I should tell her!

She stares at my skirt, her eyes practically popping
out, as if she's never seen anything like it. Although the
sun is setting and the light is fading fast, the sequins
still shine. I suppose it looks like a vaudeville costume
to her. Her purple dress comes down to her knees, and
now that she's turned my way, I can see that an apron
is covering the entire front of it. Wherever I am, I'm
definitely not wearing the right clothes.

I try to speak, but nothing comes out. My sister
would never believe that I'm actually speechless!

"You must really miss your parents right now," the
girl continues, "but Max told us they'll arrive in a few
days. I hope you'll like staying with us. By the way,
I'm Rebecca. Did Max tell you that I want to be
a performer, too?"

I still don't know where I am or how I got here,
but just then, a door opens onto the roof, and an older
man steps out. He's wearing a loose white shirt and
baggy pants with suspenders and is holding two
small pails.

Rebecca leans close and whispers, "Uh-oh.

It's grumpy Mr. Rossi, the janitor. He's doesn't like kids up here."

The janitor scowls at her. "I tell you before, Rebecca—no feeding the pigeons!" He shakes one of the pails, making a dry swishing sound. "*This* is food for birds," he adds, speaking with a thick accent.

Peering in, I catch a glimpse of birdseed. The other pail holds water.

The janitor turns to me, practically gaping at my clothes, and his eyes narrow. "Not from around here, are you?" he asks. I shake my head. "Well, I make the rules here, and the first one is no kids pestering my pigeons! Go on, both of you!"

Rebecca and I are starting to leave when Mr. Rossi looks me over again and asks, "Wait—where you from?"

"I, uh, I'm from New Jersey," I stammer.

He sets the pails down and folds his arms across his chest. "So, you must be Millie Santini, my old friend's neighbor." *Who?* Mr. Rossi keeps talking in an accent which I'm guessing is Italian. "I sent a letter to my friend and say I no gotta room here, but maybe the letter didn't get there fast enough." He frowns.

"I'm sorry your family having troubles, and worrying about the kids getting sick, but me, I no gotta space for you." He gestures toward the pigeon cages. "With so many birds I got enough hungry mouths to feed."

Now Rebecca looks uncertain. She turns to me. "Is Mr. Rossi right? Did you come all the way from New Jersey? Or are you Daisy, the vaudeville performer Max told us about?"

I hesitate. The one thing I can't say is that I'm from—well, about one hundred years in the future! I mean, I don't want them to think I'm crazy.

I know I'll need a place to stay. It would be exciting to say that I'm a performer, but what if I have to prove it?

To say you need a place to stay,
turn to page 19.

To say you are a vaudeville performer,
turn to page 24.

I really haven't done much performing on my own yet," I explain. "In fact, I'm still taking dance lessons."

"We have a lot in common, then," Rebecca says. "Cousin Max told me I have real acting talent, but I have no way to show it. You're so lucky that you get to take dance lessons. I'll bet you're going to make it big." She smiles at me, and I smile back. Rebecca barely knows me, and yet she already believes I'll be a success. If I can get over my fear of being alone onstage, I might live up to her expectations.

"As for me," Rebecca continues, "I can only dream of being in a moving picture someday."

Rebecca's brother Victor snickers. "You really are dreaming if you think you'll ever be a movie star," he teases. Rebecca's confident smile fades.

"Beckie is going to be a teacher, which is a respectable career for a young lady," her father declares.

Rebecca slumps down in her chair. It must be extra hard when her family doesn't share her goals. If I became a great tap dancer, I'm sure that at least my parents would be proud to see me perform.

After supper, the twins ask permission to walk to the

candy shop. Rebecca's father hesitates, but then agrees
that my visit makes this a special night.

"Just this once, all the girls can go together," he says.

Rebecca's broad smile returns. "You're my lucky
star," she laughs. I may have brought her a bit of good
luck, but I know I'm no star. I've got a long way to go.

We walk to Delancey Street, and soon we are sitting
on stools in a charming shop, drinking something that
Sadie calls a Raz-Lime Rickey. It tastes fruity and sweet
and tart all at once, and it's so fizzy, the tiny bubbles
make a layer of froth. I sip through a paper straw and
listen to a jazzy ragtime song playing on a windup
phonograph. It's just like one I saw in a museum, except
that this one is shiny and new. The music sounds a
bit tinny, like the sound track of an old movie. When
the song ends, the man behind the glass counter steps
to the phonograph, changes the record, and winds it
up. An old song I danced to in my tap class starts to
play: "Give my regards to Broadway, Remember me to
Herald Square . . ."

"I know this song!" I exclaim, starting to hum along.
Rebecca and her sisters start singing, and I'm glad I can
join in.

Leaving the candy shop, Sadie and Sophie walk ahead, arm in arm, and Rebecca and I follow. Suddenly, she stops and points to a poster in a store window.

"Look at this!" she exclaims. "There's an audition tomorrow afternoon at the Coronet Theater. The winner gets five dollars and a spot in a vaudeville show." She's breathless with excitement. "This could be your big chance." Then she hesitates. "But the theater is way uptown from here, near Times Square. I don't know how you'd get there."

"I've been there with my mother many times," I say. "From here I think you can just head straight up Broadway." Rebecca brightens, but I instantly regret my words. What am I thinking? Do I want to perform in front of an audience in an actual vaudeville theater? It's nothing like dancing with a class, when you've rehearsed for weeks on end. Still, I have to be ready for my solo at the next recital. I can't be so nervous about performing alone if I ever want to be a success.

Rebecca clasps her hands together in delight. "Your family will be awfully proud if you win. You're so lucky, Daisy—I'd give anything if my family would let me perform in a show."

My mouth goes dry. I've said too much already. How can I refuse now? Rebecca's trying to help me, and if I turn this down, she'll never understand.

To agree to perform at the amateur show, turn to page 38.

To find an excuse not to perform, turn to page 43.

Well, yes, I—I did come all the way from, uh, New Jersey," I stammer. "And I will, um, need a place to stay."

Rebecca gives me a friendly smile. "Well, it sure is nice to have a girl my own age in the building, even if it's just for a few days," she says. "Maybe you could go to school with me."

"Never mind about school," Mr. Rossi says to me in a crabby tone. "You gotta go back home."

I'm not so sure I'd want to stay with him anyway. At least I have the Russian dolls to take me back. "Don't worry about me," I tell Mr. Rossi. "I can get home to New Jersey by myself—really soon."

"Sure, you found your way here, now you can find your way back."

"Wait," Rebecca says, stepping closer. "We can't just send you away like that. You should at least have dinner, and a good night's sleep before you travel again." She turns to the janitor. His frown deepens, but he still doesn't offer to let me stay. "You can stay with me," Rebecca says. "I'll have to ask my parents first, but it'll just be for a day or two, until you can get back to New Jersey."

"Sure, sure," the janitor says, waving his hand in the air. "But just for a coupla days. Remember, no boarders allowed."

"We understand, Mr. Rossi," Rebecca assures him. She takes my hand and leads me toward the door. We leave the janitor to feed his pigeons, and head downstairs. A sense of excitement and curiosity bubbles up in my chest, wondering what Rebecca's family will think. Will they be as welcoming and generous as she is? Or will they be as cranky as Mr. Rossi?

I tuck the nesting dolls safely into my purse. I don't want anything to happen to them, or I'll never get home again.

Rebecca notices the dolls. "I have a set of Russian nesting dolls, too!" she says. "I named one of them Beckie—that's my nickname. I take that doll with me whenever I need some good luck."

I smile at her. "Mine bring me good luck, too." *At least they have so far,* I think. After all, I'm here on a grand adventure because of them. And I've made an interesting new friend—Rebecca!

We walk through a door in the hallway and enter a large kitchen with an ancient gas stove and a wide

white sink. It looks as though Rebecca's family has just cleaned up after dinner. They all turn and look at me with astonishment, their eyes glued to my clothes. I think my sparkly skirt is a shock to them.

I study each member of the family as Rebecca explains the situation. As I listen, I can barely keep from staring at two older girls who are identical twins. So Rebecca has twins in her family, too! There's a boy who looks just a bit older than Rebecca, and a cute little brother with huge brown eyes.

Once she hears the story, Rebecca's mother looks quite concerned. "I heard that whooping cough is spreading around New Jersey," she says. "No wonder your family wants you to stay here for a while. These outbreaks seem to happen regularly, and I guess 1914 isn't going to be any better than last year."

Did she say this was 1914?

Rebecca's father, who has a dark mustache and thinning hair, rubs the side of his face, as if thinking over the situation. Then he smiles kindly and says, "You'll be safer staying with us, but you'll have to attend school so that you don't fall behind. We'll try to get you into Beckie's classroom."

Rebecca looks a bit uncomfortable. "Mr. Rossi said no boarders are allowed. He said Millie can only stay one or two days."

"Nonsense," says her father. "She'll stay as long as necessary." I'm so pleased, I can barely keep from pumping my arm and yelling, "Yes!"

That night, Rebecca finds a warm nightgown for me to borrow, and we huddle under the covers in her bed. I hear the squeak of metal springs every time we move and feel the softness of a feather pillow under my head.

"I'm afraid your school is going to be really different from mine," I say. "Do you think I'll fit in?"

"You will if you wear one of my school dresses and a pinafore," Rebecca says. "Your fancy skirt would definitely make you stand out."

I almost ask Rebecca what a pinafore is, but I don't want to let on that I don't wear one every day. I'm guessing it's a kind of apron.

"It's a good thing that I've got two of everything," Rebecca says cheerfully, "since I get all my twin sisters' hand-me-downs."

I try to fall asleep, knowing I'll need a lot of energy tomorrow. I'm excited to see what school was like one

hundred years ago, but nervous, too. Will I do any better in Rebecca's class than I do in my own?

❦ *Turn to page 28.*

I decide to stick with Rebecca, who at least seems kind and friendly. It's a nice change from what I left behind in the antique shop. I swallow hard. "I'm a—performer," I tell her, shifting my dance bag on my shoulder. Of course, I'm not a vaudeville performer, but if you count the recital, then in a way, I will sort of be one soon.

Rebecca beams and takes my hand. "I'm so excited that you're going to be staying with us," she says, leading me toward a stairway.

"Remember," the man warns us, "boarders not allowed, so you not gonna stay more than a coupla days."

"Don't worry, Mr. Rossi," Rebecca says. "Daisy is meeting up with her family soon to join a vaudeville troupe. Isn't that wonderful?" Mr. Rossi shakes his head, as if it doesn't sound wonderful at all, and moves off to feed the pigeons.

We walk down a dark stairwell with flowered wallpaper and a wooden banister. I'm picking my way down the stairs when I'm startled by a sleek cat that seems to come out of nowhere, bounding between my legs and nearly knocking me off balance.

"That's Mr. Rossi's cat, Pasta," Rebecca explains as white paws and black patches of fur flash past. "She's a great mouser."

My new friend keeps chatting. "Someday I'm going to be a moving picture actress."

"Moving pictures?" I ask. "Do you mean movies?"

"Some people call them that," she says. "I've already decided that when my name is on a marquee, it's going to be Beckie Ruby. Do you have a stage name, too?"

I'm not sure how to answer. At this moment I almost feel as if I've stepped into a play and am taking on a new role. "I've heard that lots of actors change their names to something catchy," I begin, "but, well, I guess Daisy is my stage name."

"That's swell," Rebecca says with a smile.

"Swell?" I repeat. That's a new one on me.

"Sure," Rebecca says. "It means terrific."

"Oh," I say with a laugh. "In New Jersey, we say awesome."

"Ooh, I love new words," Rebecca gushes. "I'll use that with my older sisters. For once, I'll know something swell—I mean *awesome*—before they do."

We enter an apartment where a large family is

gathered in a small kitchen. There's a tall cabinet, a low white sink, and a long table. I don't see a refrigerator, or a dishwasher, or even a counter. I breathe in the delicious aroma of freshly baked bread.

Everyone turns to face me, and I blush from the sudden attention.

"This is Daisy," Rebecca announces. "She's the vaudeville girl that Max told us about."

A woman in a long skirt, apron, and high-necked blouse steps forward. "Welcome to our home," she says kindly. "I'm Mrs. Rubin, and this is my husband." A man with thinning hair and a trim mustache nods at me. He sets his newspaper on the table and shakes my hand. I can't miss the bold headline on the front page: *German Sub Torpedoes British Cruiser.*

Submarines and torpedoes? Is there a war between England and Germany? Then I notice the date: October 17, 1914.

I try to hide my shock as Rebecca's mother contin-ues introducing me to the family. "These are Rebecca's sisters, Sadie and Sophie." The teenage girls are identi-cal twins, and I can't tell them apart at all. Megan and I look different enough that most people don't even

know we're twins, and I like it that way.

"This is Victor," says Mrs. Rubin, nodding at a lanky boy who looks a few years older than Rebecca. "And this is our little Benny," she says, as a small boy gives me a sweet smile.

"How exciting to be in vaudeville," says Sadie. At least I think it's Sadie. "We love those shows, but we like moving pictures even more. We read every issue of *Stars Weekly* that we can get." I've never heard of this magazine.

"Are you famous?" Benny asks. Without taking a breath he adds, "Will you put on a show?"

"Not tonight, Benny," says Mrs. Rubin. "Daisy needs some time to get settled." I breathe a sigh of relief.

Rebecca beams at me. I'm afraid she's expecting me to tell some amazing stories about life in the theater, and now her brother wants a performance. How can I possibly keep up this charade?

Turn to page 33.

In the morning, Rebecca pulls a tweedy dress from a tall cabinet and hands it to me. She chooses the same one for herself. I forgot that she has two of every outfit! Then she hands me a long white apron and puts on a matching one over her dress. So, I was right about a pinafore being an apron.

It's prettier than I imagined, with frilly edges around the armholes and at the hem. I tie a bow at the back of the long white pinafore, just like Rebecca. Then I tuck my nesting dolls into one of the large patch pockets. I don't want to go anywhere without them—they're my ticket home!

Next we put on thick stockings held up with ribbon ties. The stockings are kind of itchy. Modern tights are warmer, and lots more comfortable. But it turns out that the stockings are the easy part. Rebecca holds out a pair of high-top shoes and says, "I hope these fit you." I tug them on and wiggle my toes. They're not bad. But there's a long row of tiny buttons and narrow slits for buttonholes. How on earth do I fasten them?

I study what Rebecca is doing. She pushes a shiny metal hook through the buttonhole, grabs the button with the loop at the end, and pulls it through. It looks

tricky—this will be my first test of the day. When she finishes, she hands me the hook. I'm slow, and fumble a bit, but Rebecca doesn't seem to notice. At last, I've buttoned a row of twelve tiny buttons on each shoe— much harder than tying a shoelace!

After a hurried breakfast of rolls and milk, Rebecca's mother hands us our lunches and we set off for school. There are loads of kids walking along the sidewalk. No one has a bike, and no one gets a ride. Everybody walks. It's like a kid parade!

Once we arrive, Rebecca introduces me to one of her friends. "Rose, this is Millie. She's from New Jersey, and she's staying with us for a while."

Rose straightens the two braids hanging over her shoulders. "So, already you speak English?" she says with a heavy accent. I nod, and Rose smiles. "Is lucky for you," she says.

We don't stay outside with Rose or any of the girls jumping rope or tossing balls. Instead, Rebecca brings me to a huge wooden door and together we pull it open.

"First, you have to register," she explains, and we walk into an office with a high counter. She greets a secretary and asks for the proper registration forms.

The secretary asks why my parents are not with me, and I pretend I'm too shy to answer.

"This is highly irregular," the woman insists, but eventually she sends me off with Rebecca to her classroom. Rebecca's teacher, Miss Maloney, complains about having to fit in another student. The class is large—there must be at least forty students crammed into one huge room.

We stow our lunches and wool scarves in a small open cubby set in a large wall of wooden compartments. The boys sit at desks on one side of the room, and the girls on the other.

Reluctantly, Miss Maloney moves another student so that I can sit near Rebecca. Both the chair and the desk are bolted to the floor! I can only slip in and out of the seat, but I can't move the chair any closer.

Before class begins, Miss Maloney walks up and down the rows inspecting each student's outstretched hands. I see what's expected just in time and hold my hands out, too.

"Good hygiene is important for good health," the teacher says. She stops at the next student's desk and orders, "Go scrub those fingernails, young lady!" The

girl blushes and hurries out. I notice that Miss Maloney also checks everyone's head. "Lice check," Rebecca whispers, and just the thought makes my head itch. Thankfully, I pass both inspections.

Next, Miss Maloney takes attendance. "Barofsky. Casatelli. Elovich. Filipov. Fitzgerald." The names aren't so different from the names at my own school, but as each student answers, "Present!" I hear many different accents. I relax a bit, realizing that other students are almost as new here as I am. They probably don't know the routines very well yet, either. But they're still way ahead of me.

"Sergei Rogenetsky," Miss Maloney says, stumbling a bit over the name. When a boy answers, Miss Maloney asks him to stand at his desk. "Your name isn't American enough," she declares. "From now on, your name will be Sam Rogen." The boy begins to protest, but Miss Maloney gives him a stern look. "You may be seated, Sam," she says, making a note in her attendance book.

The boy sits back down, looking confused. I wonder if he's upset to have Miss Maloney change his name without even asking whether he agrees. What

will his parents say when they find out?

Miss Maloney continues with the roll call. "Millie Santini," she says, but no one answers.

I feel Rebecca poke my arm, and I look over at her, confused. Miss Maloney walks to my desk and asks, "Don't you speak English yet, Millie?"

≈≈ *Turn to page 35.*

R ebecca's mother gestures to an older couple. "These are Rebecca's grandparents, Mr. and Mrs. Shereshevsky. They live in the apartment upstairs."

Mrs. Shereshevsky's gray hair is pulled into a bun at the back of her head, and she's frowning at me. Her husband has a white beard and wears a black skullcap. He looks me over without a word, his mouth tight. I can only wonder what they think of my outfit.

"*Oy!*" exclaims Rebecca's grandmother. "Such a nice girl—but performing on stage?" She shakes her head. I don't seem to be making a very good first impression.

We file into the dining room. Rebecca places a plate, an embroidered cloth napkin, and gleaming silverware in front of me. I only take small portions of food, since I'm an unexpected guest and this family is so big. I can't imagine having four brothers and sisters. Just trying to get along with Megan is more than enough for me.

"Tell us all about your act," Sadie says over dinner. "What's your special talent?"

All heads turn toward me, and I can feel that embarrassing blush coming back. "Well, I—I'm a tap dancer," I mumble.

Rebecca claps her hands together. "Have you met

the Astaires?" I shake my head. Rebecca rattles on. "They're a brother-and-sister dance act. They're really young, and already big stars. Maybe you'll run into them at one of the theaters where you're performing."

Could she be talking about the famous Fred Astaire? I've seen him dance in some old movies, but I never knew he had a sister.

"Where are you playing next?" asks Rebecca.

I gulp, and try to pretend that I'm just swallowing a spoonful of soup. Everyone is waiting expectantly to hear my answer. Should I name the theater where my recital will be held? I don't know if the Rubins will have heard of it or if it even existed in 1914, but maybe that doesn't matter. But if I come right out and admit that I've never been in a vaudeville show in my life, I know it will be a real letdown for Rebecca. She thinks she's meeting a showbiz pro!

❧ *To admit to never having performed in vaudeville, turn to page 15.*

❧ *To give the name of the theater, turn to page 49.*

I snap to attention, realizing that *I'm* supposed to be Millie Santini. "I'm—I'm—sorry," I stammer. "I do speak English."

Miss Maloney taps her ruler on my desk. "See that you pay better attention from now on," she says.

After taking attendance, Miss Maloney stands at the front of the room and says, "I expect that you have all mastered your times tables by now."

My stomach sinks. Why did I think that going to school with Rebecca would be any easier? Can't I ever get away from times tables?

"Sarah Goldstein," the teacher begins, "please start us off with the two tables."

A tall girl with a large ribbon tying back her blonde curls begins to recite. "Two times one is two. Two times two is four. Two times three is six." As she continues, I think how lucky she is to get an easy number to multiply. Even I know the twos. When she finishes, the girl slides back into her seat, looking relieved.

Miss Maloney continues calling on different students, and the next three recite flawlessly. "Very good," she says, looking pleased. When she calls on a boy to give the six tables, he stumbles when he gets to six

times seven. "Um, um . . . It's, uh . . ."

"Forty-two!" another boy calls out.

Miss Maloney whips around and glares at him. "Otto Holbein, keep still and wait your turn. You know better than to answer for someone else." The boy's face goes pale, and he looks down at his hands. "I'll excuse you this time, but don't let it happen again." She surveys the class, as if making sure that everyone understands the rule.

My heart pounds as Miss Maloney continues with the sevens, and then she comes to Rebecca's desk. "Rebecca Rubin, please recite the eight tables."

Rebecca stands up straight and zips right through. She's as smart as Megan! I shrink down in my seat a bit, hoping the teacher will skip me and go to someone else. Surely, she wouldn't give a new student the hardest times table on her first day, would she?

"Millie Santini, please recite the nine tables."

I breathe a bit easier, until the girl sitting behind me gives me a nudge, reminding me that *I'm* Millie Santini! My knees feel weak as I stand.

"Nine times one is nine," I begin. At least I know that! "Nine times two is eighteen. Nine times three is

twenty-seven. Nine times four is . . ." I fall silent, stuck already. My head is bursting as I try to settle on the answer. Is it thirty-two? Thirty-five? Rebecca looks at me sympathetically, as if she wants to help, but we both know she can't say a word.

> ❧ *To get Rebecca's help,*
> *turn to page 40.*

> ❧ *To guess the answer without help,*
> *turn to page 50.*

I can't let my worries about freezing onstage spoil this opportunity. I tell myself I'll do it to show Rebecca that I can, but deep down, I know I'm really doing it to prove it to myself. The longer I put off performing alone, the harder it will be.

That night, I snuggle in with Rebecca under a puffy quilt that looks like it was hand-stitched from different bits of cloth. Rebecca has lent me a nightgown that is gathered at the sleeves and the neck. It's soft and warm.

"Thanks for lending me a nightgown," I say.

"I have lots of clothes because of all the hand-me-downs from Sadie and Sophie," she says. "They always dress alike, so most of my clothes are twins, too!" I smile at the idea. Megan and I always wear different outfits. She likes her jeans; I like everything sparkly.

Rebecca's sisters whisper to each other in the bed they share on the other side of the room. I try to tune out their voices and finally share my decision with Rebecca. I know that if I agree to try out, I can't change my mind.

Before I say anything, Rebecca murmurs, "You've just got to audition tomorrow. I'll go with you and cheer you on!" Then she falls silent. I hear her sigh.

"Except I'm not sure my parents would want me to go to a theater alone."

"You wouldn't be alone if we went together," I say. "I'll audition if you come." Rebecca squeezes my hand, which is just the encouragement I need. I'm positively terrified at the idea of dancing onstage, and having a friend along might make it easier than going there alone.

"At least your parents are rooting for you to be a performer," Rebecca whispers. "Are they working on a family act?"

I find myself repeating something I've heard my father say many times. "Show business is a tough life. My parents would rather have me study hard, like my sister. I think they'd rather see me dance for fun than try to make a living in the theater."

Even if my parents were vaudeville performers, like Daisy's, I'm sure they'd agree. As for me, I'm not ready to give up my plan just yet!

◎◎ *Turn to page 55.*

look desperately at Rebecca. She slowly holds out her fingers, and I try to figure out her hint without hesitating too long.

I begin again to stall for time. "Nine times four is . . ." I glance across the aisle casually. Rebecca flashes three fingers, and then rests both hands on the desk top, extending six fingers. "Thirty-six?"

Without warning, Miss Maloney smacks a ruler against the closest desk. The girl sitting there nearly jumps out of her chair.

"Rebecca Rubin! You know the rules. You and Millie will both stay in during recess and clean the erasers and the chalkboard."

She calls on another student, who begins to recite the nine tables from the beginning. As soon as Miss Maloney's back is turned, a boy sitting across the aisle grins at me and then mouths, "Dummy!"

Why didn't the teacher see that? I fume silently.

After lunch, the rest of the class files out for recess, while Miss Maloney hands Rebecca and me rags and tells us to start cleaning the chalkboard and the erasers.

"I'm sorry I got you into trouble," Rebecca says as we clap chalk dust from the erasers through an open

window. Dust billows into the air in white clouds. "I was only trying to help."

"I know," I tell her. "This would never have happened if I had learned my times tables already. I feel like I'm the one who got you into this mess. I've tried to memorize the times tables," I admit, "but I'm just awful at them. The nine tables are the hardest."

"I know a trick that makes the nine tables simple," Rebecca says confidently. "You take away one number from the multiplier. So if it's 'nine times three,' your answer starts with 'two.' The second number of the answer is whatever makes the first number add up to nine. So, nine times three is two-seven, or twenty-seven. Nine times six is five-four, or fifty-four. It's like a game!"

At first I don't understand, but I think it through carefully, and all of a sudden, something clicks in my brain. I stop wiping the chalkboard and run through the higher numbers in my head. It works perfectly. I do know my nine tables!

"You're the best teacher ever!" I exclaim, grinning.

To my surprise, Rebecca looks away. "My parents want me to become a teacher," she says with a little

sigh. "But they don't understand that what I want is to act in movies, like Max." She turns back to me. "Here's what my grandfather says." Shaking her finger in the air, she says in a deep voice with a thick Russian accent, "'Ect-ing is no-good life for young lady!'"

I can't help laughing at what a good actress she is. "I want to be a dancer," I admit, "but my parents say I'm not being practical. But whatever I do, it won't involve arithmetic. So why do I need to know times tables?"

"Actually," Rebecca says, "they can be pretty useful no matter what you do."

Turn to page 44.

I'm not ready for the stage," I tell Rebecca.

"Why not?" she asks. "Don't you perform all the time?"

I take a deep breath and tell Rebecca my deepest fear. "I might freeze onstage." She lifts her eyebrows in surprise. "It happened to me last year," I admit. "I got so nervous standing there with the audience staring at me, I couldn't dance. In fact, I couldn't move. Someone had to come onstage and lead me off. I was so ashamed that ever since then, I've been afraid to perform."

Rebecca tries to hide her disappointment, but I can see it in her face. She becomes serious and says, "Sometimes, the more I put off facing something, the worse it gets. For now, maybe it will help if you did your act just for me. I'll be your practice audience."

❧ *Turn to page 52.*

After school, Rebecca's mother sends us on an errand to buy potatoes, onions, and carrots. She hands Rebecca a small coin pouch. I grab my own purse, putting my nesting dolls back inside.

"You know which peddlers to go to on Orchard Street," her mother says. "Be sure not to pay too much! Take Benny with you so that I can get ready for Shabbos."

I give Rebecca a puzzled look.

"Shabbos means Sabbath," she explains. "We always have our best dinner on Friday night, to start off the day of rest." She grabs Benny's cap from a hook and hands it to her little brother. "Stay close to me," she warns, "or you'll get lost." He looks worried and reaches for Rebecca's hand.

We walk several blocks and arrive at a bustling street packed with peddlers selling everything imaginable from their carts. Some have bananas and apples; others have carts piled high with everything from books to handkerchiefs. Rotted vegetables litter the street, and old newspapers blow under the carts, catching against the wheels. People push and jostle each other as they move along, and I hear shouts and laughter. Compared

to this, the jumbled antique shop I just left behind seems neat as a pin. I stick close to Rebecca and Benny, afraid I'm the one who might get lost.

Rebecca navigates the area easily, marching right up to a peddler. "I need six large potatoes, Mr. Schwartz," she says, "and no sprouts on any of them!"

The peddler fills Rebecca's shopping bag. "These are seven cents apiece," he says.

Rebecca has already figured out the total. "Forty-two cents?" she asks, her voice rising. "I'm not paying more than three cents each."

Mr. Schwartz staggers against his cart, but Rebecca ignores his dramatics. She bends down and gives Benny a loving hug. "Don't worry, little man," she croons, "we won't let you go to bed hungry tonight." Benny looks up with sad eyes and bats his eyelashes.

I feel terrible. I must be the extra mouth causing the shortage of food for dinner. But Rebecca gives me a secret wink.

"So, you need to buy potatoes, and I need to sell," Mr. Schwartz concedes with a shrug. "I'll let you have them for six cents each."

That seems pretty cheap to me, but Rebecca isn't

done bargaining. "Five cents," she insists. The peddler whistles. Then he holds out his callused hand and Rebecca counts out the change.

As we head off to buy onions, she grins. "So how much did I save?"

I multiply six potatoes times two cents. "You saved twelve cents!" Around here, I realize that means a lot.

"See?" Rebecca says with a laugh. "Multiplying comes in handy." I have to agree.

I think of my mother angling for a good price on the mirror. Like Rebecca, it seems she won't give up until she's paying what she thinks is fair. "Maybe I could try bargaining at the next stop," I suggest. "I've never done it before."

"Sure," Rebecca says. "I'll be right next to you in case you need a little help."

We walk to a cart piled with onions. The peddler eyes me sharply. I hope I can strike a good bargain. I reassure myself that Rebecca will step in if I need help closing the deal.

"Look, there's Rose," Rebecca says suddenly. She waves her arm and calls out to her friend. Rose waves back to us and motions Rebecca toward her. "Can

you hang on to Benny and buy half a dozen onions?" Rebecca asks, without waiting for an answer. "I'll be right back." She hands me the coin pouch, and I drop it into my purse. "Be sure to bargain so that we have enough left for the carrots," she cautions as she leaves.

My throat feels dry as I turn to the peddler. I wasn't planning on doing this alone. "How much are the onions?" I ask politely.

"For the best onions on Orchard Street," the man says, "only five cents apiece."

Benny squirms, and I grip his hand tighter. I can multiply the fives tables easily, so I know that comes to thirty cents, which sounds reasonable. It's the exact price Rebecca paid for the potatoes. At the same time, I realize I don't know how much Rebecca has given me.

"Don't move," I tell Benny. "I need both hands." I open my purse and search for the coin pouch but can't find it in the jumble of things I have inside. The peddler taps his foot impatiently.

Balancing my purse on the edge of the cart, I fish around in it until I find the coin pouch. I count the coins while trying to guess how much we'll need later for carrots. I think there's enough money, even without

bargaining. But if bargaining is the normal, expected thing to do, I wonder if the first price a peddler asks is always too high. Should I just pay what the peddler asks and be done with it?

Other customers crowd around, tired of waiting their turn. I try to keep a close watch on Benny and not get pushed aside.

"That's too much," I tell the onion seller bravely, but I don't sound as confident as Rebecca did. "How about, um, three cents apiece?" I try to make a sad face like Benny did, but the peddler ignores me. I guess I'm not nearly as cute as a little boy with big brown eyes.

"We can't wait all day," says a thin woman behind me. More customers squeeze forward, and I'm starting to feel trapped. This is harder than I thought. No wonder it's taking my mother so long to buy the mirror!

"I'll give you four cents each," I quickly offer. I reach for my purse to count out the change—but the space on the cart is empty. I look around frantically. My purse is gone!

∂◕ *Turn to page 72.*

Since I've already gotten myself into a pickle letting them think I'm someone I'm not, I don't want to make things worse by making up a theater that doesn't exist. I think it's best just to name the theater where my recitals are held, even though it's just a tiny little place.

"The only theater in New York where I've danced onstage is called the Band Box," I say truthfully.

"That must be off Broadway," Sadie says, and I nod in agreement. *Way, way off Broadway,* I think to myself.

I steal a glance at Rebecca. Can she guess that I haven't done any vaudeville acts at all? I wonder if I'm going to have to tell her, but I hope I won't. Thankfully, the twins start talking about movies, and I'm off the hook—at least for now.

꩜ ***Turn to page 52.***

I stumble through nine times four and nine times five, guessing both answers correctly, but when I get to nine times six, I'm stuck.

Miss Maloney gives me a moment, but soon loses patience. "You need to study and catch up to the class, Millie," she says. Then she turns toward the side of the room where the boys sit. "Leo Berg," she calls, "please stand and complete the nine tables."

A chubby-cheeked boy with his hair slicked down jumps from his seat and races through the rest of the numbers. He's fast as lightning, and every answer is correct. When Miss Maloney turns her attention back to me, Leo puts his fingers in the corners of his mouth, pulls his lips down into an ugly face, and sticks out his tongue. Miss Maloney sees nothing of this, and since she's already talking to me again, I don't have time to think about how nasty Leo is.

"Let's try again, Millie," says Miss Maloney. "This time use multiplication to answer a problem. If Mr. Smith earns forty cents an hour, and works twelve hours in one day, how much does he earn?" I feel the blood drain from my face. Is Miss Maloney picking on me because my math is as shaky as my hands are right

now? Or is she trying to help me learn?

Rebecca shoots her hand into the air and waves it around. She knows the answer already! Maybe she's just trying to keep Miss Maloney from focusing on me, but the teacher ignores Rebecca until she gives up and lowers her hand. Miss Maloney crosses her arms across her chest and says, "Millie?"

My brain struggles to find the answer. In a tiny voice I guess, "Forty-eight cents?"

"Well, you've lost some money at work today, Millie. You may sit down."

She turns to a boy hunching down in his seat. "Sam Rogen," she calls, and the boy sits bolt upright. "Can you tell us the correct answer?"

Reluctantly, the boy stands, his hands clutching the back of the chair in front of him. "I am not understanding this problem," he says with an accent.

She calls on another boy, who answers confidently, "Four dollars and eighty cents, ma'am."

I realize with embarrassment that I forgot to add on the zero!

꩜ *Turn to page 62.*

That evening, Rebecca's father leaves to get a newspaper at a nearby store, and Victor goes out to meet up with some friends. Her grandparents return to their upstairs apartment. Rebecca's mother and sisters put away the last of the supper dishes as Benny zooms a wooden car back and forth across the kitchen floor.

"Come into the parlor," Rebecca says quietly. "This is a perfect time for you to show me your dance act. It's just us, so it doesn't matter if you make a mistake." We move the chairs to the side of the room, and Rebecca settles onto the sofa to watch.

I'm not nervous at all with just Rebecca watching. I get into position, count the opening beats in my head, and hum along to my dance number. I may not be a professional, but I'm eager to prove that I do know how to tap-dance! At the end of the routine, I take a bow, and Rebecca claps enthusiastically. I hear more applause behind me and turn to see that Benny, the twins, and Mrs. Rubin are all crowded in the doorway. I didn't know I had such a big audience.

"Bravo! It's wonderful!" Rebecca exclaims, and she makes me feel happy all over. Benny hugs my arm,

and I give him an affectionate pat on the head. I hadn't expected—or even wanted—an audience, but it's nice to have a fan!

"Say," Rebecca says to the others good-naturedly, "this was supposed to be a private rehearsal. Now everyone clear the stage!" She claps her hands, and they disappear back into the kitchen.

Once we're alone again, she sits next to me and leans in close. "I have an idea," she says, her eyes gleaming. "I don't know one step of dancing, but I can sing and I love to act. Maybe we could create our own musical performance with dancing, acting, and singing all in one show, and we could perform it as a surprise for the family."

"I'd love to do that," I tell her. "And if you'd like, I can teach you a few simple dance steps, too."

Rebecca beams. "Let's start after school tomorrow. I'll have to do my chores first, though." Then her smile fades. "And I have to take care of Benny. What am I going to do with him around?"

"Benny can be in the play, too," I say, noticing that he's peeking into the parlor again.

"Yippee!" Benny shouts, rushing in and leaping

around. "I'm going to be in a musical play with a real dancer!"

"Shh!" Rebecca says. "It's a secret."

"We'll be in it, too!" the twins say in unison, popping in to join us. Clearly they've been eavesdropping. Isn't there any privacy in this apartment?

But all I say is, "Sure—the more the merrier."

"Smooth!" say Sadie and Sophie. I've never heard that expression before, but it sounds like they approve.

੦੭੭ *Turn to page 57.*

he next morning I put on my own clothes while Rebecca gets ready for school. Before she closes the wardrobe door, she hands me a white apron.

"I think Mama and Bubbie, my grandmother, are going to keep you busy with chores while I'm at school today," she says. "You'd better wear one of my pinafores so your fancy skirt doesn't get dirty." I slip my arms through the openings, and Rebecca ties it on with a bow at my back. The edges have a bit of a ruffle, and I feel as if I'm putting on a costume. It's a great way to hide my modern skirt.

"I'm going to help a friend after school," Rebecca tells her mother when we sit down for breakfast. She fiddles with her napkin, twisting it in her hands, and I can tell she's nervous about her plan. She doesn't look her mother in the eye, but she's not fibbing. I really do need her help for the vaudeville audition.

"Don't be late," Rebecca's mother warns as she sets out fresh hot rolls, butter, jam, and warm milk. "Remember, it's Friday."

Rebecca takes her lunch box, and I follow her to the stairs. The twins are already out the front door, and Victor's still at the table, scarfing down one last roll.

I'm glad I don't have to go to school, but the thought of the audition this afternoon is gnawing at me. I hope I'll find some time to practice my routine later.

As we stand together on the front stoop, Rebecca turns and points down the street. "Tompkins Square Park is just about two blocks from here," she says. "Meet me there at two-thirty. We'll have to hurry to get to Times Square in time for the audition." She heads down the stairs and then looks back at me. "Don't forget your tap shoes!" My stomach clenches. Can I really do this?

☙◦ *Turn to page 59.*

W hen we're in bed that night, Rebecca whispers, "Let's try to think of a story first, and then make up some songs and dances to go along with it."

"We could pick a fairy tale," I suggest.

"That's a great idea," Rebecca says quietly, adding, "It sure is nice to have someone my own age to share everything with. Sadie and Sophie always leave me out. They're allowed to go to picture shows with their friends, while I get stuck at home. And Benny's cute, but it's hard to do anything with him underfoot."

"I know exactly what you mean about your sisters," I agree. "I have a twin sister, and she's always bossing me around, and telling me all the things I don't do as well as she does—like arithmetic." I pause, and then add, "But she can't dance a step!"

I listen to Sadie and Sophie giggling in their bed across the room, and I feel a pang of loneliness. I wonder why Megan and I aren't that close. I'd get along with her better if we could agree on doing more things together—just as Rebecca and I are planning our play. For now, Rebecca and I are working together like best friends.

I fall asleep imagining the musical, and how

Rebecca and I are going to make it up all by ourselves. And I decide that I'm going to see if Megan would work on a play with me when I'm back home. Maybe she's just been waiting to be asked.

⟳ *Turn to page 66.*

Mrs. Rubin is busy with lots of housework, even though it's a small apartment. There's no dishwasher and no washing machine. Just when I'm wondering how she does laundry for such a big family, I spot a huge metal tub under the kitchen sink with an old-fashioned washboard leaning inside. It must take hours of scrubbing to wash everyone's clothes!

As we put away the butter and milk, I discover that the refrigerator is a small square box at the bottom of a tall cabinet. A thick block of ice in a compartment at the top keeps things cool.

Rebecca's mother asks me to play with Benny while she cleans. Benny pulls me into the living room, which he calls the parlor, and I look around for something to do. There's no television, no radio, and I know there aren't any video games.

"Let's play hide-and-seek," Benny says.

I close my eyes and count to 100 while he scurries around the apartment looking for a place to hide. "Ready or not, here I come!" I call. Although I can hear him squirming under Rebecca's bed, I pretend to look in lots of silly places, just to keep the game going. "Are you in the wardrobe?" I say loudly, opening and closing

the door. "Hmmm . . . are you hiding in the trunk?" I noisily flip open a wicker trunk at the foot of Rebecca's bed, then slam the lid. "Nope!" After a few more tries, I pull up the side of the quilt, peer under the bed, and cry, "There you are!" Benny squeals with laughter.

After a few rounds of this, where I am always the one to count and Benny is the one to hide, he takes out a box filled with jacks and a small red rubber ball. He brings me back to the kitchen, where the floor is smooth. I haven't played any games like this since I can remember. It's actually lots of fun playing jacks with Benny, and trying to do better with each turn. Behind us, Rebecca's mother is mixing dough. She covers the bowl with a soft cloth and sets it on the table.

The morning passes quickly, and after lunch, Benny is tucked in for a nap on the living room couch. I'd read him a book, but I don't see a single one. Instead, I make up a story about Tom Thumb until Benny's eyelids droop and he falls asleep.

Back in the kitchen, I see that the rising dough has pushed the cloth into a rounded mound. I am impressed as Mrs. Rubin kneads dough and then twists strands of it into a braided loaf. "Can I try?" I ask.

She nods. "Do you help your mother make bread?" she asks. "Although I suppose she doesn't have enough time to do baking, with all the performances."

"Well, she does stay pretty busy with work," I say, as Mrs. Rubin divides the dough. Then she shows me how to roll out three even strands and braid them together.

"This is hallah," she explains. "We have it every Friday. It's made with eggs, and it's sweeter than the bread we eat every day." I like the feel of the soft dough, and wonder if I could try this at home. There must be recipes for making braided bread, although I don't see any cookbooks in the Rubins' kitchen.

I look at the clock ticking on the mantel in the parlor and realize it's nearly two-thirty. I didn't get a minute to practice my routine, but I don't want to be late!

ം *Turn to page 69.*

I'm relieved when it's finally time for lunch and recess. Rebecca leads me up a long flight of stairs, and I'm surprised to find a large play space on the roof. Some girls are jumping rope, boys play catch, and hopscotch squares are chalked on the roof surface. Rebecca's friend Rose comes over carrying a jump rope. At least that's something I am good at! As we each take one end of the rope, I ask Rose about Sam.

"His real name is Sergei," Rose explains. "He's from Russia, just like me. In school, teachers don't like any name that doesn't sound American. If the teacher doesn't like, she changes! So Miss Maloney decides Sergei is now Sam." Rose looks thoughtful. "As for me, when I come to America, I am Rifka. Then I go to school, and by the time I come home, I am Rose!"

Back in class, I think about all the ways new immigrants have to change. I know that the school is trying to help the new students become more American, but still, it must be so difficult for them. I think again about the arithmetic problem Miss Maloney gave me this morning. Maybe she's especially trying to help newcomers like Sergei. When he gets older and gets a job, he'll be better off if he doesn't make the mistake I did

in calculating his paycheck! If he's good at multiplying, he won't be cheated out of what he's earned.

After school, Rebecca's mom gives us a snack of homemade bread and jam. I'm amazed that she bakes the family's bread every week. I'm used to having sliced bread that comes in a bag. The homemade bread is so much tastier! It's crusty on the outside and chewy inside. I could eat the whole loaf!

While we're eating, Rebecca asks her mother if she knows anything about Sergei, the Russian boy in her class.

"Yes, I met Mrs. Rogenetsky at the synagogue," Mrs. Rubin says. "She told me Sergei's father still hasn't found a job. I am putting together a basket of food for them now. Would you and Millie take it to them?"

Rebecca and I agree, and Mrs. Rubin writes down Sergei's address. Then she hands us a heavy basket, and we head out to find the apartment.

Rebecca leads the way to a neighborhood packed with rundown apartment buildings that she calls tenements. As we walk, Rebecca tells me about her

cousin Ana, who is still in Russia.

"Jewish people are leaving Russia as fast as they can," she explains. "There are lots of new laws that say Jews can't live in the cities, or work at certain jobs, or go to school. And now, Russia is in a war. Sergei's family was lucky to get away, and Ana's family has to get out before it's too late."

"That's terrible," I say with concern. "Is there anything you can do to help?"

"Well, Papa is sending his brother whatever money he can spare, and I'm helping out in the shoe store so that he doesn't have to pay someone to work. I wish there was more I could do to help Ana's family buy ship tickets to America," Rebecca says. "Helping Sergei's family will make me feel a little bit better." She looks around the unfamiliar neighborhood. "But I can't do anything until we find his building."

We walk down a side street, looking at the numbers on the buildings. All the front stoops are packed with kids, many of them girls my age and younger who are minding even younger children.

Rebecca shows the address to one of the girls, who points to a building just down the street.

I stay close to Rebecca as she opens a splintery wooden door and we enter a dark hallway. Wallpaper peels off the walls in ragged curls, and smells of boiled cabbage and garlic fill the stairwell. It becomes darker as we climb all the way up to the fourth floor.

᠙᠗ *Turn to page 74.*

As Rebecca gets ready for school the next morning, I wonder what I'm going to do all day without her. I'm not left wondering for long, though.

"Mama thought you could help Bubbie, my grandmother, with her housework," Rebecca says as she's getting ready to leave. I must look a bit worried, because she adds quickly, "Bubbie's really sweet, even though she seems a bit gruff sometimes."

Sure enough, Rebecca's mother sends me upstairs to help out. I knock lightly on the door, and Rebecca's grandmother opens it, holding a bottle of furniture polish and a clean cloth. I know I'm probably not going to be able to clean things well enough to satisfy her, but I try to at least be polite.

"Good morning, Mrs. Schara—shira—," I mumble nervously. I can't even pronounce her name correctly! Not a good start.

"Is hard name for Americans, I know. Since you stay with the family, please to call me Bubbie. In the Old Country, is not just for your grandmother, but for older woman you know well. Maybe you don't know me so well yet, but I am definitely old!" A smile crinkles the corners of her eyes, and I relax a little.

She looks doubtfully at my outfit. "You know how to polish?"

"Umm, I've dusted before, but I'm not so sure about the polish," I confess.

"So instead, start with the doilies," she says, pointing to the lacy needlework decorating the armchairs and the tabletops. "Through the window, give them a good shake. Me, I'll do the polishing." She puts some oil on the cloth, and while I shake out the doilies, she rubs every wood surface until it shines. Next, she shows me how to clean the carpets with a long-handled contraption that sweeps up the lint with little brushes. I have to go over the same pieces of lint a dozen times before they're picked up. How much easier it would be if she had a vacuum cleaner!

As we clean, I think about the musical play that Rebecca and I are planning. "Cinderella" might be perfect. Benny could be the handsome prince. I bet he'd like that. But would Sadie and Sophie be willing to play the mean stepsisters?

"You are here, but your head is in other places," Bubbie says. "What you are thinking?"

"Well," I say, "actually, I was thinking about stories."

"Ah," says Bubbie with a nod. "When I was a little girl growing up in Russia, I always like stories about the witch, Baba Yaga."

"I haven't heard those stories before," I tell her.

She motions me to the sofa and sits down next to me. Then she surprises me by hunching up her shoulders, wrinkling her face into a grimace, and cackling, "Here is Baba Yaga!" She begins to tell the tale of two children who get lost in the forest and end up at Baba Yaga's hut. The witch plans to eat them for supper, but by befriending some birds and a cat, the children find a way to trick Baba Yaga and escape.

"That's sort of like 'Hansel and Gretel,'" I say. In fact, I'm thinking that Baba Yaga might make a more interesting play than Cinderella. I can't wait for Rebecca to get home from school so that we can start rehearsing. But which fairy tale should we do?

❦ *To suggest doing a play about Baba Yaga, turn to page 78.*

❦ *To suggest doing a play about Cinderella, go online to* **beforever.com/endings**

A fter the loaves are laid out, I tell Rebecca's mother I'm going outside, retrieve my tap shoes, and hurry to find Tompkins Square Park. My hands are sweating as I wait for Rebecca, even though the weather is cool. I don't know how I'm going to get through the audition. It feels even scarier than the recital performance. After all, this is a professional show with an audience of strangers.

I'm relieved when Rebecca runs up to me. "Let's go," she says, and we walk as fast as we can toward Times Square.

When we arrive, I cannot believe it's the same place that I walked through with my mother yesterday. There are no digital billboards, no flashing lights, and no crush of taxis. Instead, I see sidewalk vendors selling hot chestnuts, men in bowler hats dodging between horse-drawn carriages and sputtering motorcars, and women in long dresses and wide-brimmed hats. It's still a jam of traffic, but like nothing I've ever seen before.

"There's the Victoria Theater," Rebecca says, as we approach an ornate building. "Look at the marquee. The Castles are dancing there tonight!"

"Who are they?" I ask.

"Irene and Vernon Castle?" Rebecca asks, sounding incredulous. "Surely you've heard of them. They're the most famous couple dancing on any vaudeville stage in America. The Victoria only books the top acts," she explains, "but even that theater is starting to show moving pictures."

"I just saw a movie last weekend," I say, before remembering that "movies" are brand-new to Rebecca. I stop before I say anything else. What would she think if I told her that movies are everywhere, including on our televisions, phones, and tablet screens? I couldn't begin to explain all this, even if I wanted to!

Rebecca says, "I know it seems unbelievable, but Max says it won't be long before all the theaters show moving pictures."

I nod in agreement. "I think he's absolutely right."

Rebecca checks the address of the theater where the audition will be held. "I think we go that way," she says, pulling me across Broadway. We dodge the carriages, and I'm scared to death that we're going to be run over by a trotting horse. When I get home, I'll appreciate crosswalks more than ever!

A few blocks up, we turn onto a side street, and then go left down a narrow alley. Soon we see a dingy theater that's barely visible in the dim shadows. There's cardboard covering one of the windows on the heavy front doors and crumpled flyers blowing in swirls on the sidewalk. I hope this isn't the theater advertising the audition!

I look up at the marquee. Some of the black letters are missing, so it reads: **Stage A ditions Fri ay 3 PM** Above it, a faded painted sign says **Coronet Theater**. My heart sinks, realizing this dark and dingy building is it.

"Well, it sure isn't the Victoria," Rebecca says, "but maybe it's a good place to start."

Now I'm wondering if I want to do this at all.

✑ *Turn to page 76.*

try to stay calm, but I can hear the panic in my own voice as I ask Benny, "Are you holding my purse?" I look at the peddler. "It was here just a second ago!"

"I don't have it," Benny says. "Maybe it was that boy."

"What boy?" I ask, bending down close to Benny.

"I saw a boy reaching toward the cart," Benny says. "I thought he was stealing an onion." He tries to peer through the crowd, but then shakes his head and shrugs. "I can't see him."

"What did he look like?" I ask.

"He was really skinny, and taller than Victor, and he was wearing a gray cap."

Standing on tiptoe, I look over the heads of the people around me. I think I see a skinny boy in a gray cap pushing through the swirls of shoppers.

"Rebecca!" I shout frantically. She rushes over, leaving Rose behind. I struggle through the knots of shoppers, trying to keep an eye on the thief while I explain what happened. Rebecca grabs Benny's hand and all three of us start running after the boy.

My mind flashes back to what was in my purse.

There was Rebecca's coin pouch, and the money I brought, some tissues, a comb, a pad and a pencil, a packet of extra taps for my dance shoes and . . . the nesting dolls! As soon as I realize that I've lost something more important than money, I go faster than ever, bumping into people without stopping, and leaving Rebecca and Benny behind. Now I'm truly running for my life.

The thief dashes under the elevated tracks of a rumbling train. I can feel the overhead cars rattling my bones. My hands are shaking with anger and fear. Just as I begin to catch up, he darts through a rowdy gang of older boys hanging out on the corner. I can't get around them, and I'm not sure I have the courage to push through, even to save the dolls.

∾ *To push through the boys,*
turn to page 81.

∾ *To stop and wait for Rebecca,*
turn to page 98.

ebecca walks down the hallway, finds the right apartment, and knocks.

The door opens a crack, and Sergei peeks through. "Better not to come," he says. "Baby brother very sick." Rebecca holds up the basket of food, and Sergei opens the door a little wider and takes it, nodding gratefully.

"I'm so sorry about your brother," Rebecca says. "My mother wanted to send over a few things. There's bread, and noodle kugel, and fried fish, and there's vegetable soup in there, too. I hope it helps."

Suddenly, we hear the sound of wracking coughing, followed by a high-pitched whoop, as if someone is gasping for air. Sergei turns in alarm, and I see his mother rush toward another room. The next sound we hear is weak crying, as thin as whistling.

"Doctor has come," Sergei reports, "and baby can spread sickness." As we stand there, Sergei's mother comes back into the kitchen and stands near the door. Dark shadows ring her eyes.

"You are kind," she says, "but quick you must go." She starts to close the door, and we step back.

"Is there anything we can do to help?" Rebecca asks.

Sergei's mother hesitates, and then asks in broken English if we will take a message to her daughter, who works at the hat factory. "Is emergency," she says. "Must tell about sick baby."

Rebecca looks at me, and I nod my agreement. "Don't worry," she assures Sergei's mother, "we'll do it."

Through the narrow opening in the door, I see Sergei's mother wash her hands with dark brown soap, write a hasty note, and slip it through the crack in the door. "Thank you," she says.

Just before we leave, I catch one last glimpse of Sergei's face. He looks pale and frightened. He must be worried about his baby brother, and about catching the illness himself.

∽◦◯ *Turn to page 84.*

ebecca takes my hand, and we step cautiously into the dim lobby. It's a beehive of activity. Performers rush around, pulling on wigs and tugging costumes over their street clothes. A ballerina in a long white dress pirouettes in a corner, and a juggler tries to toss oranges and apples in the air without losing them. Instruments are tuning up with a mix of sour notes.

In the middle of the lobby, a man shouts out orders like a circus barker. He's wearing a derby hat and a brown suit that's too small to button over his potbelly. Bushy sideburns and a drooping mustache nearly cover his face. "Get yer number here," he yells, waving cardboard numbers in his hand. "No audition without a number!"

Rebecca bravely guides me through the crowd until we're standing in front of the man.

"No kiddie acts without a grown-up," he snaps at us. "Come back some other time with your parents."

Looks like I won't be auditioning after all. My chance to prove I can perform alone seems sunk, but in another way I'm almost relieved that I don't have to prove it right now.

But Rebecca isn't put off. "Her parents are on their way," she declares, grabbing a number and quickly handing it to me. Then we lose ourselves in the crowd.

༺ *Turn to page 86.*

The day passes quickly, and by the time Rebecca returns, I've thought of a great reason to choose the Baba Yaga story. As soon as we're alone in her room, I tell her, "I know Bubbie doesn't approve of you wanting to become an actress, but she might be really pleased to watch us perform the Russian folktale she told me today."

"That's a great idea!" Rebecca says enthusiastically. "I think that might win over my grandparents and my parents. But let's keep it a secret until the last minute, so it's a surprise."

Back in the kitchen, Rebecca announces to her mother, "We'll take Benny up to see the pigeons."

"Be sure to keep a close eye on him," Mrs. Rubin cautions. "Don't let him get too close to the wall around the roof."

We dash up the stairs and follow Benny out into the sunshine. The pigeons are cooing, probably hoping that Rebecca has brought them some bread crumbs. But she's completely focused on the play. "Bubbie has told us lots of stories about Baba Yaga," she reminds Benny. "You know all about the witch in the forest, don't you?"

"I 'member her house has chicken legs," Benny says

earnestly. "It walks around the forest."

"That's right," Rebecca agrees, "and we're going to make up a play about her. How about if I pretend I'm Baba Yaga, Daisy will be a girl in the forest picking flowers, and you'll be her little brother. While she picks wildflowers, you search for strawberries. Then you both get lost and end up at Baba Yaga's hut." Benny nods, wide-eyed.

Rebecca instantly takes on the role of the witch, scrunching her face into a wrinkly scowl. She waggles her finger at Benny, and then at me, singing out orders in a cackling voice.

"Fetch the water, spin the thread, or I'll bake you into bread!" Rebecca takes a breath, thinking quickly, and then sings another line. "Fill the bucket, turn the spinner, or I'll eat you both for dinner!"

Is she just making this up on the spot? She's really good!

Benny backs away, and even I feel a little shiver as Rebecca finishes her made-up song. I try to get into my role, and pretend I'm holding the handle of a bucket.

"Oh, dear little brother," I say with alarm, pretending to look inside, "there's a hole in the water bucket!

How will we ever bring enough water to Baba Yaga?"

Benny looks worried, and peers into the bottom of my imaginary bucket. "Baba Yaga's going to eat us up!" he cries. He looks genuinely frightened. Is he just acting?

"Don't worry, little brother," I reassure him. "I know exactly how we can fool the witch and get back home." I try to remember the story that Rebecca's grandmother told me. "If we're kind to the birds and the black cat, they'll help us get away."

Benny's face is pale. My suggestion about finding a way to let the cat and the birds help us escape from Baba Yaga doesn't seem to help at all. Benny looks as if he's ready to burst into tears.

✹✹ *To stop the production,*
turn to page 90.

✹✹ *To help Benny thwart the witch,*
turn to page 116.

here's no time to waste! I push straight into the middle of the group and am almost through to the other side when a husky boy with red hair blocks me. He puts his hand on my shoulder, and my heart races.

Instead of giving me a hard time, as I feared, he looks at me with concern. "What's wrong, lass?"

I point toward the thief, who is now disappearing into an alleyway. "He stole my purse!" I cry.

Without another word, the redheaded boy takes off after the thief, and I try desperately to keep up, but I fall behind and lose sight of both boys.

Finally, I have to stop. I lean against a building and try to catch my breath. I've lost everything—Rebecca's money, my money, and worst of all, my nesting dolls. How will I ever get home again? I like it here—at least, I like being with Rebecca—but I don't want to have to live here forever. I need to get back to my own life, and my own family.

Suddenly, through the tears that spill down my cheeks, I see the redhead striding toward me—holding my purse! The instant he hands it to me, I frantically look inside. The coin pouch is gone, along with the

money I had with me when I came. Left behind are the tissues, the notepad and pencil, and the extra taps. But I don't see the most important thing—the nesting dolls. My eyes are blurred by tears as I pull everything from the purse, letting it all fall to the street. They're gone! I'll never see my parents or Megan again. I sink to the ground, sobbing.

"Oh—I found this lying in the alley," the boy says. "Is it yours?"

I wipe away my tears and see that he's holding out my precious wooden dolls.

"How can I thank you?" I manage to choke out, standing unsteadily. "If there was any money left, I'd share it with you."

" 'Twas nothing," he says. "Sorry I couldn't snag the purse before the thief robbed you." As Rebecca and Benny catch up, and the boy sees I'm safe with them, he jogs back to his friends.

I can barely face Rebecca. "I've lost the money your mother gave us. I'm so, so sorry!"

Rebecca wraps her arms around me. "It's not your fault," she reassures me. "We lost the change, but at least you and Benny are safe. We can manage without

the carrots and onions." She glances down. "At least you still have the dolls, although they didn't bring you much luck today."

I'm clutching the nesting dolls for dear life. "If I'd lost these, I'd never be able to replace them." I look at Rebecca and try to make her understand, without giving away the whole truth. "They're my—connection to my family."

She nods sympathetically, and we pick up all the things that I'd let fall. Benny reaches for my hand, and with Rebecca's arm around my shoulders, we head for home.

❦ *Turn to page 91.*

When we get back down to the front entry, a man in a dark suit is nailing a sign to the outside of the door. "No school for you tomorrow," he says as he walks off.

I look quizzically at Rebecca, and we both step up to read the sign.

"Warning," it says. "Whooping Cough in Building."

Rebecca smothers a little cry, her hand over her mouth. "Sergei's baby brother has whooping cough! And to think you came to New York to get away from that same sickness!"

I look at the note in my hand and realize with a shock that although Sergei's mother washed her hands, I might already be exposed.

Instead of thinking about herself, as I am, Rebecca says, "I hope Sergei doesn't get sick, too. And now he's going to miss weeks of school before he's allowed back." Gently, she takes the note from my hand and unfolds it. "It's written in Yiddish," she says. "It's warning Sergei's sister, Edna, of the illness and telling her to find a friend to stay with until the danger is past."

I never heard of whooping cough before Rebecca's mother mentioned it when I arrived. Now that I realize

I could catch it, I'm scared. Suddenly I want to get back home—now.

Rebecca seems to guess what I'm thinking. "I'm sorry you got caught up in this," she says. "You don't have to come with me to the factory."

I wish I could shake off my fears and stay here a little longer with Rebecca, but I'm overcome with the urge to get home. Maybe my father knows of a modern medicine that can keep me from getting this horrible disease.

ꝏ *To go home now,*
turn to page 93.

ꝏ *To go to the factory,*
turn to page 110.

A young man who I guess must be a stagehand leads us to the back row of the theater, along with several other performers.

"You can watch the acts that go on before yours," he says. "Someone will get you when it's time for you to be backstage." Then he disappears up the dark aisle.

The theater is packed, and the people in the audience stomp their feet, clapping in rhythm and yelling, "Show! Show! Show!" This is nothing like the friendly families that come to my recitals!

Rebecca and I settle into tattered velvet seats. As the stage lights flicker, my heart flutters, too. What have I done? I don't want to let Rebecca down, but the thought of dancing alone on that stage feels more and more terrifying.

"Here comes Mr. Walrus," Rebecca says lightly, as the man with the drooping mustache steps onto the stage. He raises his hands to silence the crowd. It doesn't quite work, so he shouts above the noise.

"Ladies and gentlemen, welcome to the Coronet Theater extravaganza—where you choose the featured acts. We have an array of talented performers, and at the end of the show, we'll line them up and let

you vote with your applause. The winner takes home five silver dollars and gets a spot in our next show!" He holds up a velvet bag tied with a blue ribbon and gives it a shake. Then he holds up a second bag and announces that the runner-up will win three silver dollars. The audience roars with approval as the coins clink.

He introduces the first act, and the performer struts onto the stage. It's an acrobat who tumbles through a fast routine with back handsprings and one-handed cartwheels. A band seated below the stage tries to improvise a musical accompaniment. Next, the juggler performs, now dressed in a pointy hat and a multicolored outfit with bells hanging from his sleeves. He tosses vegetables and fruits into the air. Suddenly, he misses. A tomato splats onto the stage, and an orange smashes down. The crowd boos.

The walrus man steps from the wings and extends a cane toward the juggler. He hooks the man's arm and pulls him off. The crowd howls with laughter. How humiliating! Stagehands rush out and mop the floor. My stomach lurches. If I make a mistake, could I get the hook, too? That would be even worse than

freezing up. I'd die of embarrassment, and Rebecca would surely be ashamed to admit she even knows me, let alone that she brought me here.

One act after another takes the stage—an opera singer in a long gown sings in a high, shrill voice; a woman with a herd of costumed dogs puts the animals through their paces; a comedian dressed in an outlandishly oversized outfit tells jokes with a heavy accent. I feel sorry for him when nobody laughs. Instead, a man in the audience starts heckling.

"Why don't you learn English?" he shouts.

"What? You got a problem?" the comedian calls down to the man. He suddenly switches into another language, his hands gesturing in the air. The audience erupts in laughter.

Rebecca leans close. "That's Yiddish," she says. "The comedian says he knows what it's like to come to America and try to find a job so that you can pay your rent. Then he says that just today, on his way to the theater, he saw his brother running up the street. He yells, 'Why are you running?' His brother hollers back, 'I'm trying to keep two men from getting into a fight!' So he asks him, 'Which men?' And the brother

answers, 'The landlord and me!'"

It takes a second for me to get the punch line, and when I do, I chuckle. I guess vaudeville is full of silly jokes.

The last act in the group is a sister act. Two young girls dressed in frilly bonnets and long prairie dresses with ruffled pinafores begin to sing a hymn, "Ave Maria," in sweet sopranos. The audience melts, and the women especially seem to be absolutely cooing over these little girls.

The next group of performers is summoned from the back row. That includes me. My heart is beating so fast I can practically hear it. I take Rebecca's hand. I'm not budging without her!

✐ *Turn to page 95.*

ime out!" I call, putting my arm around Benny. He's trembling a little. "I think this is just a bit too scary," I tell Rebecca. "Maybe we need to choose a different fairy tale."

"It's such a good story, though," Rebecca says, "and it will really please Bubbie." She bends down close to Benny. "I have an idea. How about if *you* play Baba Yaga? Then you won't feel afraid."

Benny's eyes grow wide. "I can be a mean witch!"

We start rehearsing again, and Rebecca and I pretend we're sisters caught by Baba Yaga and made to work for her. Benny becomes a super-mean witch. He even tries singing Rebecca's song. "Catch the water, spin me thread, or I'll spread you on my bread!" Rebecca and I stifle our giggles and let Benny play the role the way he wants.

After rehearsing the rest of the afternoon, we're ready to put on our play. We herd the entire family into the parlor to spring our surprise. I'm on pins and needles, wondering if they'll love the show—or not.

❧ *Turn to page 108.*

As soon as we enter Rebecca's kitchen, Benny is bursting to tell the family about the purse-snatcher. He jumps around to demonstrate how he was the one who saw the boy running away.

"And Millie was really brave!" he adds. "She ran right through a bunch of big boys to chase the thief." He tells about the redheaded boy who got the purse back.

"I know where those ruffians hang out," Victor, Rebecca's older brother, says knowingly. "They don't even go to school. They just fool around all day, blocking the sidewalk and acting tough."

"But one of them helped me," I remind him.

"Not everyone is lucky enough to go to school," says Rebecca's mother. "Things can't be easy for them, and will only get harder."

I never thought about what I'd be doing if I didn't go to school, or what my future would be like. All the times I complained I'd rather be dancing, I guess I wasn't looking at the big picture. I always wished my mother would stop telling me to be more like Megan and focus on my schoolwork, the way she does, but now I wonder if my sister has it right. I'm going to

think of school differently from now on.

That evening, Rebecca's entire family sits down to the Friday night dinner. It's so different from my family's hurried meals. Earlier today, when I lost the dolls, I thought I'd lost the chance to ever go home again. But in this moment, as the candles flicker on the table, warm feelings wash over me when I think of getting back to my own life. When I do, I'm definitely going to make some changes. I smile at the thought. It seems as if the whole world has slowed down, just to make a new space for me.

❧ *Turn to page 96.*

R ebecca seems to sense my panic. "I think you need to go back to your family," she says.

"I don't want to just leave you like this," I reply, "but would you be angry with me if I went home now?"

"If I were you, I'd want to go home right away too," Rebecca says with concern. "I'll deliver this note while you head back to the apartment and get your things. I know my parents will understand."

I can tell without talking that we are going to miss each other. I turn and begin walking away from Rebecca, but just as I do she turns her head for one last look, and we wave a sad good-bye.

Back at Rebecca's apartment, Mrs. Rubin seems concerned. "I never would have sent you over to Sergei's if I'd known you and Rebecca could be exposed to whooping cough," she says. "To think you came all this way to avoid this disease, and now it's here in our own neighborhood." She pats my shoulder gently and adds, "Since you were at Sergei's such a short time, I think you'll be just fine. Still, be sure to tell your family about what happened when you get back."

In the empty hallway of Rebecca's building, I pull my nesting dolls apart and then fit them back together. I feel as if I'm reeling, but in a moment, I blink and discover I'm already back in the antique shop.

᭢᭢ *Turn to page 100.*

We head backstage, my taps clicking sharply on the wooden floor. Rebecca stands beside me in the wings as I wait my turn. I hear the audience's catcalls or applause, and sometimes a strange clattering at the end of each act. I don't know what it is until I peek out and see a stagehand sweeping up pennies. Backstage, he hands them to the performer. I guess the audience is already voting—with pennies of approval!

Then a stagehand nudges me forward. "Yer on!" he mutters. I try to move, but my feet seem as if they're planted in cement.

Rebecca whispers, "Do you want me to go out with you?"

ᴄ𝒆𝒪 *To go out alone,*
turn to page 99.

ᴄ𝒆𝒪 *To accept Rebecca's offer,*
turn to page 102.

As we get ready for bed that night, I lay out my purple skirt and my shoes. I set my purse and dance bag next to the bed, and then I climb in.

"The purse-snatching was one of the scariest things that ever happened to me," I tell Rebecca. "I need to go back home tomorrow. I miss my family too much." I'm even missing Megan.

"I can't blame you," Rebecca says. "I wouldn't be able to stay away from my family for very long, either." We snuggle under the warm blankets. Rebecca takes her wooden nesting doll, the one she calls "Beckie," from under her pillow, and I reach into my purse for my own nesting dolls.

"Even after I'm home," I tell Rebecca, "I'll be thinking about you. For one thing, whenever I'm studying my arithmetic lessons, I'll remember how you bargained with the street peddlers, and your trick for multiplying times nine."

"You taught me something, too," Rebecca says. "It was fun showing you a new way to multiply. It made me realize that maybe I would enjoy being a teacher."

I pull the covers tighter and whisper, "Luckily,

you have lots of time to decide what you want to do. Whether you become a teacher or an actress, you're going to be great."

ᘯ *The End* ৹ᘯ

To read this story another way and see how different choices lead to a different ending, turn back to page 73.

always thought my legs were strong from dancing, but right now they feel like jelly. I sag against a wall, gasping for breath. Just ahead, the boys on the corner move up the street, throwing light punches at each other as they go.

Rebecca and Benny rush up to me. "Did we lose him?" Rebecca asks anxiously.

"He got away—with everything," I say. I'm stunned at what I've lost, and I'm too exhausted even to cry.

Rebecca tries to comfort me. "There wasn't too much money left," she says. "Mama will understand." Perhaps she will forgive me, but if I can't go home again, will I forgive myself?

Suddenly, I do feel tears coming, and I can't hold them back. They roll down my cheeks, and I heave silent sobs. How can I tell Rebecca that I've lost so much more than a pouch filled with change? I may have lost my entire family.

Turn to page 105.

o, I have to do this alone," I tell Rebecca, my voice trembling. I wish she could come with me, but she doesn't know how to tap-dance. I'm petrified, but I have to prove to myself that I can do this. I'm not sure I'm even breathing as I walk to center stage while Rebecca takes a seat in the front row.

The band plays a few bars of a song I don't recognize. Suddenly I can't remember the opening to my routine. Frozen, I stare out over the darkened audience. A man yells, "Let's go, girlie! On with the show!"

Out of the corner of my eye I see movement in the wings. The walrus man is holding up the cane. Oh, no—I'm going to get the hook!

Just when I'm sure that this is going to be a bigger disaster than the recital I ruined last year, a familiar voice floats up from the audience. "Hey, that's the famous Daisy Belle!" It's Rebecca. She begins a rhythmic clapping, and the audience joins in. "Go, Daisy!" she calls.

The band picks up the tempo, and I know I have to dance—just for her.

Turn to page 113.

om!" I call, a little too loud. I rush up and wrap my arms around her waist.

"My goodness," my mother exclaims. "What's gotten into you?"

I can't hold back. "I heard something about whooping cough today. It scared me."

Mom smiles and pats my back. "Don't worry, sweetie," she reassures me. "You've been vaccinated against that disease since you were a baby."

"I have? Really?" I ask, with a rush of relief.

"Doctors are pretty important," Megan pipes up.

I feel as if a weight has been lifted off my chest, and I take a deep breath. I should have known that there would be a modern vaccine.

Then I feel a pang of concern. No one in Rebecca's time is protected. I can't help worrying about what will happen to Sergei's baby brother, and to his family. I sure hope that Rebecca and her family don't get sick.

I turn to Megan. She's smiling at me. I start to bristle, but then I realize that her smile isn't superior—it's sincere and even hopeful, as if she's genuinely pleased at my sudden interest in something other than dance.

I give her a warm smile back. If you think about it,

my sister's really pretty cool. I mean, I may not have her interest in science, but I'm sure glad there are people like Megan, and my father, who do.

∞∂ *The End* ∞∞

To read this story another way and see how different choices lead to a different ending, turn back to page 14.

Since Rebecca can't tap-dance, I don't know what we'll do onstage together. But right now I'm far more worried about stepping into the spotlight alone. I nod silently, and Rebecca leads the way.

The stagehand tries to stop her. "Hey," he says, "you're not . . ." But Rebecca boldly pushes past, and once we're out there, there's nothing he can do.

As we stand in the glaring spotlight, the familiar fear grips me and I can't seem to move. It's as though my knees are locked together. The people in the audience stomp their feet impatiently.

Fearlessly, Rebecca steps forward and announces, "Ladies and gentlemen, we're the Ruby Sisters—Daisy and Beckie. Or you can call us the Daisy Belles!" The audience chuckles. Rebecca points to me. "My sister thinks she can dance. What chutzpah!" This time the audience laughs out loud. "I can outdo her any ol' day." Rebecca extends her arm, as if inviting me to begin, but I'm rooted to the stage. Under her breath she says, "Quick! Teach me a step!"

I turn to her. Now that I can't see the audience, my knees unlock and my panic disappears. "I'll bet you can't do this," I say bravely. I perform a few tentative

steps as I recite the moves: "Lunge, back, shuffle-ball change." I end with a flourish of my arm and start to feel a little better. Maybe I can do this!

Rebecca clumps her foot down in a loud *thunk*! She shuffles a little and forgets the step. She drapes her arm across her forehead and says, "Lounge back?" The audience roars. She stands straight and drags her feet sideways. "Then scuffle," she declares. "That's not very hard!"

Sneaking a glance at the audience, I remember to put on my stage face—a big smile—as I do a few complicated steps, more confidently this time.

Rebecca's mouth drops open. "Uncle!" she cries. "I may not be able to dance, but I sure can sing." She leans over the stage and peers down toward the musicians in the orchestra pit. "Mr. Bandleader, how about a little Broadway music?" she asks. She starts singing in a strong voice that must carry all the way to the balcony, and I'm shocked at how she really can belt out a song.

"Give my regards to Broadway," she sings, just like the record in the candy shop, but with grand stage gestures. She may not be a trained professional, but her voice is pure and strong.

"Remember me to Herald Square.
Tell all the gang at Forty-Second Street
That I will soon be there."

At first I dance slowly and carefully, not wanting to mess up. Then I stand straighter and start adding every step I know, smiling at Rebecca and, occasionally, at the audience as well.

Rebecca sings louder and faster, repeating the chorus twice, with the band racing to keep up.

"Whisper of how I'm yearning
To mingle with the old time throng.
Give my regards to Old Broadway
And say that I'll be there e'er long!"

Something hits my foot as I take a bow, and then something else—hard. *Jing, jing!* It's pennies. The audience loves us!

❧ **Turn to page 114.**

"D on't cry," Benny says gently. "Maybe the robber is still hiding down there." He points toward an alley. In a flash, he takes off.

"Benny, stop!" Rebecca yells, but he ignores her. Rebecca chases after her brother and I try to keep up, but I'm several steps behind her. Just as I get closer to the alleyway, I hear Rebecca let out a sharp cry. I turn into the dark space between two rundown buildings, afraid of what I'm going to find. But instead of something terrible, as I'd imagined, I see Rebecca grinning as Benny runs toward me with his short little legs pumping, proudly waving something in the air.

"My purse!" I exclaim, wiping my eyes. I give Benny a bear hug, lifting him off the ground and twirling him around. Then Rebecca and Benny lean forward as I open the purse and rummage around inside. My stomach sinks as I realize that the coin pouch isn't there. I've lost Rebecca's money.

"I'm afraid the money your mother gave us is gone," I say. "I'm so sorry!" I truly feel awful, and I don't dare say how relieved I am to see my nesting dolls still lying in the bottom. They weren't worth anything to the thief, but for me they're priceless.

"How are we going to buy onions and carrots?" Benny asks.

Rebecca pats his shoulder. "We'll have to manage without them," she says. "There's nothing else we can do. At least we have the potatoes."

Feeling defeated, we walk away from the peddlers toward home. On the way, we pass a little boy, not much older than Benny, singing in a sweet voice to passersby, and we stop to listen. I notice that he's placed a cup on the sidewalk in front of him. A few people drop pennies into the cup, and the boy bows without missing a note.

Rebecca sighs wistfully. "I wish we could perform to replace at least some of the money we lost," she says.

Benny tugs her sleeve. " 'Member when we did a show in front of our building and earned six pennies?"

Rebecca puts her hands on her hips. "And do you remember how angry Bubbie was?" She turns to me. "Benny and I performed a singing and comedy routine, and when my grandmother saw us, she was furious. She said we were shaming the family!" Her face reddens as she tells me how she was punished.

I can understand why Rebecca is afraid to perform

on the street ever again. But I can't help thinking that it wouldn't embarrass anyone if I performed. Nobody here even knows me. And I'm the one who lost the money—why couldn't I perform my tap routine and maybe replace some of the stolen change?

꼰 *Turn to page 127.*

Ladies and gentlemen," Rebecca announces, "welcome to Rubin's Home Theater. You are about to see an original musical play!"

Rebecca's grandparents glance sideways at her parents. Are they expecting Mr. and Mrs. Rubin to call off the show?

But Rebecca doesn't miss a beat—she continues her introduction like a real emcee. "Tonight's performance is the great Russian folktale of Baba Yaga, with original songs and dances!"

Rebecca's grandfather places a hand over her grandmother's, as if to reassure her, and we start right in.

Rebecca is particularly dramatic when the witch captures her, and when we escape, I do a few tap steps with a pirouette tossed in for good measure. Benny is a pretty scary witch, but he can't help looking adorable, especially when he sings his version of Rebecca's song. From the opening to the end, the show goes smoothly, and the entire family applauds. I glance over at Bubbie, and I'm tickled when she gives me an approving wink.

Rebecca is bursting with happiness afterward. "Even my grandparents loved it," she exclaims.

"I'm so glad you came up with the idea of doing a play

of Baba Yaga. It was the perfect choice."

"When Bubbie told me that she loved stories of Baba Yaga when she was growing up, I figured it might work." I think about the connection that I've made with Rebecca's grandmother. "Maybe when your audience feels a personal connection to your show, it's more likely to be a hit."

"I'm going to remember that," Rebecca says. "Max always says that if you can make your audience laugh, they'll love you. But I think your idea is just as important. In fact, I think it might be the key to helping my family accept my dream of becoming an actress."

I beam at Rebecca. Just hearing her say that I've helped her think of a new way to earn her parents' support feels like a standing ovation!

Tomorrow morning it will be time for me to return to my own life. I miss my family, and my dance friends too—especially Liz. But I'll never forget Rebecca and our world premiere of *Baba Yaga: The Musical*.

∽⦾ *The End* ⦾∾

To read this story another way and see how different choices lead to a different ending, turn back to page 14.

If Rebecca can stay strong to help Sergei's sister, then I will, too. The factory isn't far, but we drag our feet as we walk. Neither of us talks.

When we get to the building where Edna works, there's a crowd of young women waiting to go inside and begin their shift.

"I met Edna at the synagogue last week," Rebecca says, scanning the group of workers. "I'm sure I'll recognize her." Suddenly a bell clangs loudly and the women hurry inside. "Edna!" Rebecca calls out, and a worker turns her head.

I'm surprised to see how young Edna looks. She's probably only about twelve or thirteen. Isn't she too young to be working in a factory?

The crowd surges forward, and Edna is swept along until she disappears inside the building. Rebecca shakes the note in her hand. "I've got to get this message to her," she says.

"Let's catch up before it's too late." I pull Rebecca inside, mixing with the workers. As we shuffle up a dark, creaking stairway, a humming sound, like the drone of a plane flying too low, begins to build, and I shiver in spite of the stuffy air. Then I hear the

door being bolted behind us. Feeling panicky, I grasp Rebecca's hand. She looks frightened, too.

As we round the second flight of stairs, I see a large room up ahead with wooden forms lined up by the dozens—no bodies, just heads topped with unfinished hats. The tables are littered with ribbons, bows, artificial flowers, and large pincushions that look like angry porcupines.

Rebecca works her way through the crowded hallway, pulling me along, until she is almost next to Edna.

Suddenly a man yells, "Kids into the closet!" He herds the youngest workers—who don't look much older than me—toward a narrow doorway. In the confusion, Rebecca manages to stay close to Edna until we three are squashed side by side into a narrow space with a group of girls. They all look nervous but don't say a word. Suddenly the door slams closed.

In the stifling darkness, I can barely breathe. "What's happening?" I ask, my voice squeaky with fear.

The other girls silence me with shushes. In a bare whisper, Edna says, "The foreman, he make us hide because we are under the age—understand? Workers must to be at least fourteen."

Another girl adds softly, "City inspector must be coming. If we are caught, then right away, no more job."

I stay quiet—I don't want to make these girls lose their jobs. I know they wouldn't be working here if they didn't need to.

Rebecca leans over and whispers in Edna's ear, and I hear a faint rustle as Sergei's sister pockets the note.

I lift my chin, trying to catch some air in the suffocating space. "I can't breathe," I murmur. "I think I'm going to faint." I've got to get out of this dark, airless space, and I only know one way to do it. I'm positive that none of the girls can see me as I reach inside my purse and grab my nesting dolls.

♥♥♡ **Turn to page 137.**

Hearing Rebecca's voice seems to unfreeze my feet. If only Liz would offer to cheer me on during my solo, maybe it would help as much as Rebecca's encouragement does right now.

This time, the band starts playing the notes of an old song I know well. "Daisy, Daisy, give me your answer do . . ." My feet start to move, slowly at first and then faster as the band picks up the tempo. My recital routine fits the quick beat perfectly. When I do a spin in one part, I wave to Rebecca as I turn. The audience thinks I'm waving to them, and as they clap, I feel new energy spurring me on.

Finally, I wind up the routine and take a bow. It wasn't my best performance, but I made it all the way through. And I didn't get the hook! I tap-dance my way off the stage, feeling a wave of relief.

⌒⌒ *Turn to page 119.*

Backstage after our performance, I can't thank
Rebecca enough for making the dance a
success.

"You're a natural," I compliment her. "I never
thought about giving the routine a dash of comedy, but
I think it made the Ruby Sisters stand out. It warmed
up the audience, and it warmed me up, too! Once I
heard the laughter, my dance steps came easily.
I couldn't have done it without you."

I split up the pennies the stagehand has collected
for us. Rebecca puts hers into a dress pocket, and I tuck
mine away in my purse. I notice that these pennies look
a little different. Abe Lincoln is on one side, just like at
home, but the back of the penny has a pattern around
the outside edge that looks like a stalk of wheat, instead
of a building. I guess a lot of things change over time—
even coins.

"I can't wait to find out who the audience chooses
as the best act," I say. "Do you think we have a
chance?"

"We just might," Rebecca says. Then she glances up
at a large clock on the wall and her face clouds over.
"Oh, look at the time! I've got to get home. My parents

will be so upset if I'm late—especially tonight," she frets. "And it's my job to set the table."

I'm not sure why tonight is special, but I can see how anxious my new friend is, and I owe her so much. I don't want to make her late. Still, I would love to stay long enough to find out who the winner is. It could be us!

> ≈≈ *To wait for the contest results,*
> *turn to page 120.*

> ≈≈ *To leave the vaudeville theater now,*
> *turn to page 133.*

Staying in my role, I dig into my pocket and then hold out my cupped hand, pretending something's in it. "Let's feed the birds our last bread crumbs."

Benny looks at me uncertainly, so I nudge him to the pigeon cages, where I pretend to offer the birds some bread crumbs.

"But how can the birds help us if they're in a cage?" Benny asks, with real worry in his voice.

"Oh, don't worry, these birds have special powers that the witch doesn't know about," I say as I pantomime feeding the next pigeon. I glance over at Rebecca to see what she thinks we should do next, but she is fully in her role and doesn't look up. She pretends to stir a potion in a large pot, muttering a made-up chant. She has taken off her hair ribbon and tousled her hair into a stringy mess half-falling over her face. With her eyes peering through her hair in a witchy glare, she really does look fierce and frightening. I can see why Benny is creeped out by the sudden and rather shocking change in his sister!

I turn back to him, but he's nowhere to be seen. "Where are you, little brother?" I ask. But there's no

answer. "Benny?" I call, louder this time, breaking character. "Benny, where are you?"

Still no answer.

"Cut!" I shout. "Rebecca, is Benny with you?"

She stops stirring and looks up, pushing her hair off her face. "I thought he was playing the scene with you."

"Well, he was, but—he got kind of scared. I thought he was right behind me. I don't know where he went."

She straightens up. "He can't have gone far. Benny!" she calls.

We listen for his answer, but all we hear are the pigeons cooing and the distant street noises from below.

I search around the pigeon cages, and Rebecca looks behind some weathered boards stacked in a corner of the roof near the door, but Benny is nowhere to be found. With a rising panic, I think of Mrs. Rubin cautioning us not to let Benny get too close to the edge of the roof. Rebecca must have the same sinking thought, becaue we both rush to the low wall that surrounds the rooftop. I'm frightened of what we might see as we anxiously peer over the edge. Horse-drawn wagons and cars move slowly along the street, and

people hurry along the sidewalk on their way home from work. There's no sign of anything unusual. Rebecca looks over at me, and we both let out huge sighs of relief.

"He must have just quit the play and gone downstairs," Rebecca says, "although I don't know how he could have opened the door without us noticing. I'll go check the apartment. Can you search the cellar? He could be hiding down there. You'll see the door at the end of the hall where you enter the building."

We race downstairs. I leave Rebecca at her apartment and hurry down to find the cellar.

❦ *Turn to page 122.*

When the show is over, Rebecca meets me in the front lobby. "You scared me a little in the beginning of the act," she admits, "but you sure finished with a flourish!"

I squirm at her praise. "Thanks for your shout-out," I say. "I couldn't have done it without your encouragement. I was so nervous."

"Luckily, once you got into your routine, no one could tell you had stage fright," Rebecca assures me. "You were a real trouper!"

As Rebecca and I walk back to the apartment, I promise myself that at the recital, I'm going to be Liz's cheering section. We might not be appearing in the same dances, but that's a perfect opportunity for us to give each other a boost. Maybe if I let her know I'll be in the audience rooting for her, she'll be able to do the same for me. Isn't that what friends are for?

◦◦◦ *The End* ◦◦◦

To read this story another way and see how different choices lead to a different ending, turn back to page 95.

e're almost the last act," I say. "Do you think we can wait just a few more minutes?"

Rebecca looks up at the ticking clock. "It's late, but we can't leave now. We're in this till the curtain comes down!"

After a mime with a painted white face finishes his act and takes his bows, the walrus man steps out and invites all the performers onstage for the audience's decision. Rebecca and I march out together, our arms linked.

The announcer jingles a bag of coins over each performer's head in turn, and the audience cheers and stamps, or jeers and boos. I can't imagine how the performers who get booed can stand there and smile. I'd be so humiliated, I'd probably burst into tears!

The audience claps and cheers for the woman with the animal act, and the dog she's carrying in her arms begins to howl. The two girls who sang "Ave Maria" so sweetly get thunderous applause. When it's our turn, the crowd claps wildly. I can't tell which of us got the loudest approval.

At last, the walrus man steps forward and says, "It was a close competition, but clearly your choice is—the

adorable Singing Angels!" The girls step forward, curtsying over and over. They accept the bag of silver dollars and step back into the line of performers. We didn't win, but I don't feel disappointed. I made it through without freezing, and the audience liked our act. And even though I was super nervous, performing with Rebecca was more fun than anything I've ever done. Now I'm absolutely sure I'm going to work as hard as I can to become a professional dancer.

The walrus man holds up his hands to quiet the audience. "There's one more prize," he says. "The second-place finishers, taking home three silver dollars, are . . ." He pauses dramatically while the drummer in the orchestra pit beats a fanfare. Then he cries, "The Ruby Sisters!"

I gasp, and then hold Rebecca's hand high in the air. I twirl her around a couple of times as I tap-dance to the front of the stage. We accept the prize money, bow to the audience, and dash away, filled with excitement. Out of all those talented performers, Rebecca and I won second place!

❧ *Turn to page 135.*

At the end of the first-floor hall, I find a narrow door with a rusty metal latch. The door is open just a crack. I open the door a little wider, and a dank, musty smell wafts through the opening. Cautiously, I peer into the dim basement. My heart is beating faster, and I wish I didn't have to go down into the cellar alone.

"Benny?" I call, but I hear only a faint echo of my own voice. I take two steps down the stairs, which creak under my feet. Again, I call Benny's name into the darkness, but there's no answer. I wish I had offered to check for Benny in the apartment and let Rebecca come down here.

A thin ray of light filters through a tiny window high in the wall. I can barely see, but I hear a muffled sound. I walk cautiously down the stairs, holding on to the railing to steady myself. At the bottom, the sound is clearer, like stifled sobbing, coming from a dark corner. Slowly, I move toward the noise, my heart beating so hard I wonder if the whole building can hear it!

Gradually I make out a dim figure in the corner and realize that Benny is sitting on the dirt floor, his arms around his knees, his head down, crying softly. I hurry over and kneel beside him.

"Benny? Are you okay?" I ask, resting my hand on his small shoulder. "What happened?"

"I didn't want Baba Yaga to eat me for supper, and you said the birds and the cat would help us if we were kind to them," he sobs. "But I knew the birds couldn't help, so I came down here to find Pasta. But when I picked her up, she scratched me!"

"Pasta must have been scared, too," I say. Then I hear Rebecca calling from the top of the stairs.

"I found him!" I yell.

She hurries into the cellar and sinks down next to her brother, wrapping her arms around him tightly. "You scared us," she says, and I explain about Pasta.

Rebecca checks the tiny scratch on Benny's hand as best she can. "I guess we should have told Pasta she was in our play," Rebecca jokes. Benny wipes his eyes with his sleeve but doesn't wiggle out of Rebecca's arms.

"I think your acting was too convincing," I tell Rebecca. "Even the other actors thought you were a real witch!"

Rebecca and I take Benny back upstairs to the apartment to clean his scratch.

"You're just in time for baths," Rebecca's mother tells us as she sets a metal washtub near the sink and starts boiling water on the stove. Victor brings out fresh towels for him and for Benny, and Mrs. Rubin sends Rebecca and me out. I can't imagine having a bath in the middle of the kitchen!

"Come on," Rebecca says, leading me to her bedroom. "We'll take baths upstairs in Bubbie's apartment." She chooses two fresh outfits from her wardrobe. I guess I'll soon see how things are done when you don't have your own bathroom.

"Why do you have baths before dinner?" I ask her on the way upstairs.

"It's Shabbos," Rebecca explains. "Tonight at sundown, the Sabbath begins, so we have a special dinner. Mama cleans the kitchen and the house, and we take baths and put on clean clothes. Everything looks nice and feels special. It's my favorite night of the week."

When Bubbie has the bathwater ready, I scrunch down into a metal washtub that's been placed in a corner of the kitchen near the warm stove and filled with hot water. I even learn how to dunk my head to wash my hair. I wonder what Rebecca would think if I told

her that at my house I take a shower every single day.

Later, dressed in one of Rebecca's pretty school dresses, I help her set the table with beautiful dishes, embroidered napkins, and a set of gleaming silver candlesticks. My stomach rumbles with hunger at the smell of the food.

Before we sit at the table, we all stand behind our chairs and listen as Sadie and Sophie say a blessing and light two candles. Then we pass bowls of chicken noodle soup that Bubbie ladles out from a big serving bowl. Just as we start sipping our soup, Benny's father notices the red scratch on Benny's hand.

"What happened there, Benny?" he asks.

"I was in a play," Benny replies. "Pasta was supposed to help me get away from Baba Yaga, so I went into the cellar and found her, but instead of helping me, she scratched me!" Now our secret is out.

Rebecca's mother turns to her. "While you were playing on the roof, Benny was in the basement?" She looks stern. "Does this mean you weren't watching him?"

"We were!" Rebecca insists. "He was part of the play we were making up, but then he just ran off when

we turned around for one little second!"

"It was too scary!" Benny exclaims.

"You were responsible for your brother," Mrs. Rubin scolds. "Which is more important—a play, or taking care of Benny?"

Rebecca and I steal a guilty glance at each other. Now we're in trouble.

Turn to page 143.

aybe I could do a street performance,"
I suggest. "I know a few tap-dance steps, and if
I earned the money, no one could blame you."

Rebecca's eyes dance instead of her feet. "Let's try!"
she exclaims. I do a small shuffle-ball-change step
and turn like a windmill with my arms outstretched.
Rebecca applauds.

"It's not as loud without my tap shoes, but if it
looks interesting, maybe people will still stop to
watch," I say.

"I'll collect the pennies," Benny offers, taking his
cap from his head and holding it out. "I'm good at
that."

I try to ignore the people passing by, and the butterflies flitting in my stomach. *This isn't a stage,* I remind
myself. *No one will know if I mess up and start again.*

Tentatively, I take the first step and begin to dance.
Rebecca calls out to people, "Step right up! Don't miss
a beat of those tapping feet!" Amazingly, some women
holding shopping bags and pushing baby carriages
stop. They smile, and each drops a penny into Benny's
cap. A circle forms around us, and I try not to let this
small audience rattle me.

By the time the dance is over, Rebecca says we have just enough money to buy the carrots and onions—if we drive some hard bargains.

I can't believe I performed my recital routine for real money! *Hello, world!* I think happily. *I'm a professional dancer!* If only there were some way to share this moment with my friends back home. But how? No one would believe where I am, or how I got here. At least for now, Rebecca is my friend, and she shares my excitement.

"The crowd loved you!" Rebecca says, her eyes sparkling. She squeezes my hand.

"You were part of the show, too," I point out. "You were the emcee—the master of ceremonies! You're a natural!"

Now Rebecca's eyes really gleam. "That's what cousin Max told me." She gets a dreamy look and says, "Someday . . ."

We skip back to Rebecca's apartment with Benny giggling between us. As we get closer to her building, Rebecca faces Benny squarely. "I know this was quite an adventure," she says, "but you can't breathe a word of what happened, or we'll all be in trouble."

Benny pouts. "Not even about how I found Millie's purse?" he whines.

"No," Rebecca tells him, "because then we'd have to explain how we earned back the money."

"You and I will always remember how you rescued my purse," I assure him. "It will be something special just between us." I wink at him, and Benny grins.

The dinner that evening is more than special, and the table is set with what must be the family's best dishes and linens. The twins recite a blessing over lit candles, the flickering flames creating a soft glow. Delicious noodle soup starts the meal, along with homemade bread. The chicken is the best I've ever had.

But no vegetables ever tasted as sweet as the onions, carrots, and potatoes that Rebecca's mother has pre-pared. I'm sure that I'm enjoying them all the more knowing that I earned them myself, through my very own dance performance. I know I played only a small part in getting the extra food, but it was a perfect one for me.

When Rebecca and I get ready for bed that night, she says wistfully, "I loved being the emcee today. I wish I could do more acting."

"You can," I assure her. "Think about it: You were performing today when you bargained with the potato seller. You created a little scene where poor Benny would go hungry if you didn't get a good price—and won the peddler over." I think back on the day we shared. "And when you helped me learn the times tables, I realized that you'd make a wonderful teacher—and the best teachers I've had were also performers, in a way. They taught us songs, and helped us put on plays, and sometimes acted out our history lessons. Whatever you do, I'm sure you'll find a way to use your acting talent."

I go to sleep and dream about seeing Rebecca in a movie where she sings and dances through a street filled with peddlers' carts. I wake up the next morning feeling happy all over—except for one thing. I want to go back home. I think I'm ready to do my best tap performance ever at the recital.

"I wish I could stay long enough to see you become a movie star," I tell Rebecca with a smile. "But I really miss my family."

"I knew you'd have to leave sometime," she says, "but I hoped it wouldn't be so soon."

"At home we have a code for best friends. We link our pinkie fingers and say, 'BFF.' It's a promise to stay Best Friends Forever."

"I like that," Rebecca says, extending her pinkie. We hook our fingers together and both exclaim, "BFF!"

I put on my purple skirt and pick up my dance bag and purse, patting the lump from the nesting dolls inside. I wonder if Rebecca will become a teacher one day, or if she'll hold on to her dream and find a way to become an actress. I realize for the first time how lucky I am to be able to choose whatever I want to be when I grow up.

After saying good-bye to Rebecca's family, I pause in the vestibule just inside the front door of her building. There's no one in sight. Taking the dolls from my purse, I pull them apart, line up the two halves of the larger doll, and push the pieces together. In a dizzying flash, I'm back inside the antique shop.

My mother is still at the counter, bargaining with the shopkeeper for a good price on the mirror. She's smiling, so it must be going well.

I look again at the special dolls I'm holding. The rest of the set remains standing on the display table,

and I tuck them all back together, where they belong. I wonder if I can convince the dealer to sell me the set of dolls. If she agrees, I'll bargain for a fair price first. I know just how to do it!

∞◦ *The End* ◦∞

To read this story another way and see how different choices lead to a different ending, turn back to page 37.

We'd better leave, then," I say reluctantly. "I'm not going to let you get into trouble at home after all you've done for me."

Rebecca doesn't argue, although I can see she's torn. I think she wants to find out who wins as much as I do. "We'll never make it home in time, even if we run all the way," Rebecca says. "We could take the trolley, but that costs money."

I have two quarters in my purse, but my quarters might not look right for 1914. What if the conductor noticed the date on them? He'd be shocked to see they were made almost a hundred years in the future. "How much does the trolley cost?" I ask.

"Five cents each," she says glumly.

"Let's use some of the pennies we just earned," I suggest, and she agrees. We each count five pennies from our stash and jump on the next trolley car.

"Why is tonight's dinner special?" I ask. "Is it someone's birthday?"

"Oh, no," Rebecca says. "We're Jewish, and Shabbos—the Sabbath—begins Friday night at sundown. I just can't be a minute late!"

The trolley starts up again, the bell clanging, but

with all the carriages and wagons and puttering Model-T cars at every intersection, and the trolley stopping every few blocks to pick up more passengers, we're not making much progress.

My dad loves antique cars—he'd go nuts over these! But it's hard to relax and enjoy the amazing sight of New York a hundred years ago when I see the anxious look on Rebecca's face. She's looking out the window too, but she's not admiring the cars—she's watching the street signs and biting her lip. The trolley is so slow, I almost think we could walk faster. The buildings are all in shadow, but at the intersections I can see that the sun hasn't completely set yet.

Come on, trolley driver, step on it!

◦◦◦ *Turn to page 140.*

Outside, streetlights blaze. "So this is why Broadway is called The Great White Way," Rebecca says, admiring them. I hadn't heard that before, but it's a perfect description. Everything is drenched in white light. I wonder what Rebecca would call Broadway today if she saw all the colored lights and moving billboard images that now light up every inch of the avenue. But Rebecca looks anxious. "Seeing the lights shows me how late I am," she says. "We'd better use some of our pennies to take the trolley home."

We stand at the trolley stop with our pennies in hand, but two trolleys pass us by, so full that some passengers hang onto the outside railings. Finally, the third car stops. Rebecca is close to tears, and I feel guilty for suggesting that we stay at the theater so long. At last, the trolley drops us close to East Seventh Street, and we race back to the apartment.

Inside, Rebecca's parents are pacing around the kitchen. Her father steps forward, holding out a pocket watch on a gold chain to show us how late it is.

"What you are thinking, coming so late?" Rebecca's grandmother exclaims, fussing over a frying pan.

"Dinner is getting ruined, waiting for you!"

"I'm sorry, Bubbie," Rebecca murmurs.

"Where have you been, young lady?" Mrs. Rubin demands. "You've had us all worried to death. You were expected home in time to have your bath and then set the table." Rebecca's mother gives me a quick glance. "This is the start of Sabbath," she explains, "and it's important to begin at sundown, and not a moment later."

"Victor's in trouble, too," Benny pipes up.

"Is your brother with you?" Mr. Rubin demands.

Before Rebecca can answer, the door bursts open and Victor rushes in, completely out of breath. He holds up his hand before anyone else can speak.

"I'm only late because of them," he says, pointing an accusing finger at Rebecca and me.

∾☙ *Turn to page 144.*

Just as I am about to separate the dolls, the door bursts open. Rebecca pulls me into the hallway and silently closes the door behind us. I inhale a deep gulping breath of air and look up to see the foreman waving his hand frantically. His face is red with anger.

"Whatta ya doing out here?" he demands.

"We aren't your workers," Rebecca tells him. "We were just delivering an important message. Now we're leaving."

"Out!" the foreman commands us. He points toward the stairs, just as a tall, skinny man in a rumpled suit trudges up, a clipboard and pencil in his hand. He must be the inspector. He eyes us suspiciously, but Rebecca simply nods politely and keeps walking. I follow her lead, right down the stairs and out the door.

At last, we breathe fresh air, and I feel thankful knowing that I never have to return to the hat factory. The nesting dolls are still clutched tightly in my hand.

"If Edna is discovered hiding in the closet, she'll be out of work, along with the other girls," Rebecca frets. "She's the only one in her family who is bringing in any money at all. Where will she go now that she can't

return to her tenement? I hope she has a friend at work who can take her in."

I look back at the brick building and realize that the windows are covered with cardboard, blocking out the sun. "It must be horrible working there!" I say. "Those girls are kids—just like us!"

"I know," Rebecca agrees. "But some children, like Edna, don't have any choice." Rebecca links her arm into mine, and we stay close together as we walk.

Thank goodness I do have a choice, I think, feeling almost guilty. I've never thought about what it would be like if I couldn't go to school. Studying is easy compared with working in a factory. I realize how lucky I am to be able to go to school, and to take dancing lessons with my friends. And that's when I know that I want to go back home.

I take a deep breath. "I need to go home now, Rebecca. All this has made me miss my family more than ever."

"I don't blame you," she says. "But I'm going to miss you awfully!" She holds my arm tighter and adds thoughtfully, "You know, sometimes I forget how lucky I am. My parents worked in a shoe factory as teenagers

when they first came to America. Now Papa has his own shoe store, and I'm able to go to school instead of having to work as they did."

I understand exactly how she feels.

Tonight, when I'm back at home, I'm going to master those times tables, I promise myself. *And that's just the start.*

Everything looks the same when I get back to the antique shop, but inside, I feel so different. My mother seals the deal on the mirror, and I line up the two smallest dolls on the shelf with the rest of the set.

As we leave the shop and head down Thirty-Ninth Street toward the ferry, I take Megan's hand. At first, she pulls back a little in surprise, but then she relaxes and gives my hand a squeeze. Despite chilly breeze off the waterfront, I feel warm all over.

◦◦◦ *The End* ◦◦◦

To read this story another way and see how different choices lead to a different ending, turn back to page 85.

We race up the stairs and into the apartment.

Dinner hasn't started yet, but Rebecca's mother scolds her, and it makes me feel terrible.

"Your sisters already set the table for you," Mrs. Rubin says.

"I'm really sorry," Rebecca apologizes. I wonder if she's going to tell her mother where we were. "I didn't mean to be late, but I met Daisy in the park, and—and we lost track of the time."

"Hurry along now," Mrs. Rubin interrupts. "There's no time for a bath, but you need to wash up and change your clothes. And find something suitable for Daisy to borrow." My shiny purple skirt was flashy enough for the audition, but it isn't right for this dinner. We are turning to go when Victor comes rushing into the apartment, slamming the door behind him. He's out of breath, as if he's been running.

"And where have you been?" Rebecca's father asks.

"Sorry," Victor says casually. "Something came up." He smirks at me and Rebecca, and then beats us to the sink and starts washing.

The dinner is pretty fancy, with blessings recited over a pair of candles, Mrs. Rubin's beautiful braided

bread, and a single ceremonial glass of wine. The food
is delicious, but Rebecca and I are both distracted and
can't help stealing glances at each other. I can tell she's
wondering who won the contest, just as I am. If only we
could have stayed to the very end.

After the dinner dishes are cleared and the kitchen
is spotless, Rebecca and I try to find some privacy in
her bedroom. We're not alone for more than a minute
before Victor saunters in and leans against the door
frame.

"I was almost late for dinner because of you two,"
he declares.

Rebecca squirms. "You can't blame us," she says,
trying to sound innocent. "We were in the park."

"Sure you were," Victor says in a mocking tone,
"but only for about thirty seconds. I was right behind
you, and then I was right in front of you—in the
audience!"

"Please don't tell Mama," Rebecca whispers. "I was
only trying to help Daisy audition for a job!"

"A vaudeville job for Daisy—or for you?" he asks.

Rebecca is close to tears. "I can explain," she begins,
but then Victor grins and swats her arm.

"Well, don't have a conniption!" he says. "I'm not going to tell. In fact, I really came to tell you that the Ruby Sisters won second place!" Then he shrugs. "Too bad you weren't there to pick up your prize money. The lady with the animal act came in third, and she got your prize. That's going to buy a lot of dog food!"

Victor turns on his heel and walks out. Rebecca lets out a little scream of delight. "Awesome!" she exclaims, jumping up off the bed. "Being on a real stage was awesome, too. I'd love to keep doing our sister act!"

I feel the same thrill bubbling inside me. Rebecca showed me that I can perform alone—or almost alone!—without losing my nerve. Suddenly I can't wait to get back to my own time and try to keep that courage flowing, even though I'll have to do it without Rebecca at my side.

∽⌒ *Turn to page 151.*

didn't know Benny would get so upset,"
Rebecca protests. "We were only acting."

"Acting is a big responsibility, too," says Mr. Rubin. "If you're good at it, your audience will feel as if the story is real. Tales of Baba Yaga are scary, and Benny's too young for such a frightening show."

Rebecca sighs. "I was trying to include him," she says, "because Benny hates to be left out of things. I didn't think he would get scared if he was in the play." Rebecca sounds distressed, but I see a hint of pride in her eyes. She must be thinking of how well she acted to have made Baba Yaga seem so real.

Mrs. Rubin isn't done yet. "Being a big sister is an important job. Nothing should come before making sure your brother is safe."

Rebecca looks truly sorry now. Her face is flushed, and I feel guilty, too.

ᑫᑫ *Turn to page 147.*

saw them leaving the park and followed them all the way to Times Square," says Victor. "The next thing I knew, they had gone into the Coronet Theater. I was standing at the back of the audience, wondering where they had disappeared to, when the two of them walked out and performed in the show!"

"What!" Rebecca's grandfather exclaims, as though Victor couldn't possibly be right. "Our Beckie is on a stage?"

"I didn't go there to perform," she protests. "I was only trying to help Daisy audition." Her eyes brim with tears, and my heart sinks.

"Don't blame her," I say quickly. "I needed help finding the theater, and then when it was my turn to go onstage, I froze." I hadn't planned to volunteer any information about our little escapade, but now that Victor has spilled the beans, the least I can do is try to keep Rebecca from taking all the blame. "If Rebecca hadn't joined me in the act, I would have gotten the hook instantly." I wish her family could understand her talents. "Rebecca's a natural. Because of her, the act was better than I could have ever performed by myself. We won second place—and a prize of three silver dollars!"

I take Rebecca's hand and give it a squeeze for support. We both wait for what seems like an eternity for her father to speak.

Finally, he says, "Well, Beckie, what are we going to do about this?"

In a thin voice, I pipe up. "Well, to start with, I'm giving my half of the prize money to Rebecca." It's the least I can do, and her family needs it far more than I do. I take out the huge silver coins and drop them into Rebecca's hand.

Rebecca hands them to her father. "Please put these toward Uncle Jacob's ship tickets, Papa," she says. "At least my performance will help his family come to America."

Rebecca's father clears his throat. "I'm glad to see you considering others before yourself," he says. "And I suppose—*ahem*—that's what you did when you decided to step onstage with Daisy, too."

Is there a tiny twinkle in his eye as he says this? Either way, I hope this means Rebecca has been forgiven.

Later, when we are alone, Rebecca says, "I hope you don't mind that I gave the money to Papa. He's trying so hard to save enough money to bring his

brother's family here from Russia."

"I'm glad that it will help," I assure her.

Now Rebecca gives me a mischievous smile. "You know, just between the two of us, I'm really not sorry about stepping out on that stage. I had the chance to do something I love, and I was able to help other people, too—including you!"

I smile back. Although I didn't want Rebecca to get into trouble, I can't regret our performance, either. For one thing, it taught me that performing with a friend by my side is a lot less scary than being onstage alone.

When I get back, I'm going to ask Liz if she'd like to practice with me until we both learn the dance solo perfectly. After all, why does it have to be a solo? If I help Liz master the steps, and we ask Ms. Amelia, maybe she'll let Liz and me do the routine together. Even if she doesn't, Liz will know that I wanted to share the spotlight with her. And with our extra practice, maybe Liz will get a solo next time. Then, just like Rebecca, I'll get to do something I love—and help someone else at the same time.

∽⊙ *Turn to page 150.*

In bed that night, Rebecca and I pull the covers over our heads and talk softly, hoping Sadie and Sophie can't hear us.

"I hate it when the twins won't let me join in with them," Rebecca says. "So I thought I was being nice by including Benny today, but I guess I didn't think about how young he is, and about how he might not really understand that it was all just a made-up story." She pauses. "I never would have forgiven myself if anything bad had happened to him. Benny is lots more important to me than a play."

We both fall silent, and I soon realize that Rebecca is asleep. I lie awake for a long time, thinking. I don't include Megan in most of the things I do, and she goes her own way, too. Still, I know that I'd be a wreck if anything ever happened to her. Suddenly, I miss my sister—a feeling I never expected. I reach over and take the two small nesting dolls from my purse, with the two sister dolls tucked safely together.

The next morning, I go back to my own family. I realize that Rebecca has given me an amazing gift—

a chance to make a fresh start with Megan. As soon as I get my bearings in the antique shop, I watch her for a moment, absorbed in her science book. Quietly, I stand beside her and look at what she's reading. It seems to be a chapter on trees. "You're learning about trees?" I ask.

She nods. "We're supposed to collect and identify leaves from as many different trees as we can."

I like trees. They're graceful, almost like dancers holding a pose. They're certainly more fun than times tables. A lightbulb goes on in my head.

"We could go on a nature walk this weekend," I offer. "I bet we could find a lot of different trees if we do it together."

Megan looks surprised—and pleased. "That would be super." Then she adds cautiously, "You know, I was thinking about your recital. Maybe if you practice and practice your part until every step is automatic, you won't be as nervous about forgetting it onstage. That's how I learned the times tables. When you do some-thing over and over and over, it gets tucked away in your brain for whenever you need it."

Now it's my turn to be surprised. I never thought

about dancing and math having any connection, but I think Megan might be on to something. I give her a high five, and we both grin. Maybe we're not such opposites after all.

≈ *The End* ≈

To read this story another way and see how different choices lead to a different ending, turn back to page 80.

The next morning, I'm ready to return to my own life and try out my plan for the recital. I thank the Rubins for all they've done to help me, and explain that I'll be meeting my parents in Times Square. Rebecca walks me to the trolley stop, and we hug good-bye before I climb on.

I take a seat in the back of the car, behind all the other passengers. Then I kneel down behind the seat and pull out my nesting dolls. With a tug, a twist, and one final push, the trolley car dissolves in a swirl of colors, and I find myself back in the antique shop.

Megan is lost in her book, and Mom stands at the counter, making her final bargain. Amazingly, the clock still reads 5:41 p.m. I am stepping toward the display shelf to return the dolls to their rightful place when a rack of floaty scarves catches my eye. I stop and pick out two black-and-white-flowered ones. These are going to be perfect for my next "sister act"—with Liz.

∽◦◦ ***The End*** ◦◦∽

To read this story another way and see how different choices lead to a different ending, turn back to page 115.

he family is up early the next morning, and I put on my own clothes. I hate to part with the cute, old-fashioned dress Rebecca let me borrow for Sabbath dinner, but I leave it hanging in her wardrobe and fold the pinafore neatly on her bed.

"Thanks for letting me stay," I say to the Rubins. "I loved being here, but it's time for me to leave. I'm going to meet up with my family today—and get ready for my next performance."

"I wish you could stay forever," Rebecca replies. She gives me a long hug, and as she leans close to my ear, she whispers, "Maybe the Ruby Sisters will perform again one day."

"You helped me so much," I say, so softly that only she can hear. "Even a few butterflies in my stomach won't hold me back now."

As soon as the trolley comes up the street, Rebecca waves good-bye. "I'll watch for your name on a marquee!" she calls.

The trolley stops, but instead of getting on, I duck into a deserted space between two apartment buildings. Taking the nesting dolls from my purse, I pull them apart, line up the hands on the larger doll, and

push the pieces into place. The bricks of the buildings become a swirl of red, the sidewalk spins before my eyes, and I shut them tightly. I'm on my way home. Just knowing I've gained the courage to perform, I feel that I've won something important.

⌘ *The End* ⌘

To read this story another way and see how different choices lead to a different ending, turn back to page 34.

ABOUT Rebecca's Time

In 1914, New York City was home to many *immigrants*, or people from other countries, just as it is today. Immigrant neighborhoods like Rebecca's were densely populated. People spilled out into the streets to shop, visit, and cool off during hot summer days. Children played on front stoops and sidewalks, and street vendors set up carts selling everything from food to furniture to sheet music. Life in the city was exciting and noisy—and sometimes unsafe.

Apartment buildings were crowded. In 1914, most did not have indoor bathrooms, and people washed themselves in the kitchen, where they also prepared food, which meant illness could spread very quickly.

Today doctors can vaccinate children to protect them from many diseases, but in Rebecca's day, when dreaded diseases such as polio and whooping cough struck, the best way to limit the disease's spread was to separate, or *quarantine*, people who were contagious. A placard was nailed to the door of a building to prevent visitors from coming in and those who were exposed to the disease from leaving. The city might also try to prevent large groups of children from gathering. During a terrible 1916 polio epidemic, New York City officials banned children from libraries and movie theaters! Some towns in New Jersey even refused to let families trying to leave the city get off the train cars for fear they'd bring polio with them into more communities.

Immigrants often found work in factories, where they worked long hours under difficult conditions for little pay. Although it was against the law, factories sometimes hired children to work, because they could be paid even less. When city inspectors came to make sure the factories were obeying labor laws, the children would be ordered to hide!

Although immigrants and working-class Americans like Rebecca's family didn't have much money to spend on entertainment, they enjoyed movies and shows. In the early 1900s, vaudeville was the most popular form of entertainment in America. A vaudeville show was like a variety show combined with a circus. Audiences would see a series of short acts, including singers, actors, dancers, comedians, magicians, acrobats, and even trained animals!

New York's premier theater district, Times Square, had many elegant vaudeville theaters. Their bright marquees, with thousands of electric lights, illuminated Broadway at night, giving rise to the nickname "The Great White Way." Most performers could only dream of seeing their name on the marquee at a lavish theater like the Victoria or the Palace, but some big-name entertainers got their start at small-time amateur nights. Jewish comedian Fanny Brice won a five-dollar amateur prize before becoming one of the most famous comedians in America. Brice and other stars, such as Fred Astaire and the Marx Brothers, moved from vaudeville to film as the popularity of movies eclipsed and eventually brought about the end of vaudeville.

Read more of REBECCA'S stories,

available from booksellers and at *americangirl.com*

෨෧ *Classics* ෨෧

Rebecca's classic series, now in two volumes:

Volume 1:
The Sound of Applause

Rebecca uses her talents to help
cousin Ana escape Russia. Now
she must share everything with
Ana—even the stage!

Volume 2:
Lights, Camera, Rebecca!

Rebecca gets the best birthday
present ever—a role in a real
movie. But she can't tell anyone
in her family about it.

෨෧ *Journey in Time* ෨෧

Travel back in time—and spend a day with Rebecca!

The Glow of the Spotlight

Step inside Rebecca's world and the excitement of New York City
in 1914! Bargain with street peddlers, and audition for a Broadway
show. Choose your own path through this multiple-ending story.

෨෧ *Mysteries* ෨෧

More thrilling adventures with Rebecca!

The Crystal Ball

Will a visit to a fortune teller reveal the truth about Mr. Rossi?

A Bundle of Trouble

Rebecca realizes the baby she's caring for is in danger—and so is she.

Secrets at Camp Nokomis

Rebecca's camp bunkmate seems nice, but what is she hiding?

A Sneak Peek at

The Sound of Applause
A Rebecca Classic

Volume 1

What happens to Rebecca?
Find out in the first volume of her classic stories.

ebecca Rubin tugged at her wooden doll until the top and bottom pulled apart to reveal a smaller doll nesting inside. There were seven painted dolls in all, each one tucked inside the next. They reminded Rebecca of her family, which numbered exactly seven.

The dolls had belonged to Mama when she was back in Russia, before Rebecca was born. But now the Russian dolls were Rebecca's treasure. She lined them up along the parlor windowsill, behind the sheer curtains.

"Ladies and gentlemen, your attention please!" said Rebecca to her imaginary audience. Slowly she drew back the curtains and wiggled the doll she thought of as the mother to the front of the windowsill stage.

"It's almost sundown," Rebecca said in a no-nonsense mama voice. "I hope you've all had your baths." She moved the mama closer to one of the smaller dolls. "Beckie, dear," she said sweetly, "you are so grown-up now. Tonight *you* may light the candles."

Rebecca pretended two of the bigger dolls were her older sisters. She moved them to face the mama and squawked in a high voice, "She's not old enough! She's practically a baby!" The two big sister dolls butted into

the little Beckie doll, and it wobbled close to the edge of the windowsill.

Rebecca pushed the papa doll until it stood in front of the others. "Well, curl my mustache," she said in a deep voice. "Beckie's not a baby anymore. She knows the Hebrew blessing perfectly. She is certainly old enough to light the candles tonight."

Before Rebecca could make her brother dolls speak, Mama's very real voice broke into her performance.

"Beckie, you'll have to put away your dolls," she called from the kitchen. "It's time to set the table."

"Phooey!" Rebecca said under her breath. She let the curtains fall across her dolls and turned back to the parlor. Extra leaves had been placed in the table to make room for everyone, and Rebecca smoothed the large white tablecloth. She set out two silver candlesticks and placed one white candle in each.

Every Friday, Mama cooked and cleaned all day to prepare for the Sabbath. Bubbie, Rebecca's grandmother, came down from her apartment upstairs to help cook. Before the sun set, the family came together for a special dinner. Friday night was Rebecca's favorite time of the week. *But Mama should let me do something more important*

than just setting the table, she thought as she lifted a tall stack of Mama's best dishes from the sideboard.

Mama looked in from the kitchen. "Don't carry too many plates at once!" she cautioned. "And we need one extra tonight."

"Who's coming?" Rebecca asked, adding a plate and dividing the pile in two. Through the doorway, she could see Bubbie frying fish in a black iron pan. Mama and Bubbie glanced at each other, without answering her question.

That made Rebecca even more curious to know who would be sharing their Sabbath dinner. "Who is it, Mama?"

Mama stirred sizzling potatoes and onions as she answered. "My cousin, Moyshe."

Now Rebecca nearly did drop the plates. "The actor?" she asked. She had overheard her parents talking about Moyshe before, but she had never met him. He usually traveled around the country, acting in vaudeville shows, but other times he was out of work and needed to borrow money from Papa. Rebecca had always wondered what an actor was like in real life, when he wasn't onstage. Tonight she would find out.

Rebecca took special care setting the table. She folded the linen napkins so that the crocheted edges were lined up neatly. If a real actor was coming to dinner, she wanted everything to be perfect.

"Sadie! Sophie!" Bubbie called. A few strands of gray hair slipped from her neat bun and framed her round face. She opened the oven door and slid out two braided loaves of *hallah* bread. Bubbie only baked hallah for Friday nights and holidays. Each loaf needed two eggs, and eggs were expensive.

Rebecca's twin sisters hurried in, wearing matching dresses. Sadie's eyes sparkled, and she looked eager to help. Sophie followed behind her.

"Come check if hallah is done," Bubbie instructed them.

"But the loaves are so hot," Sophie complained. She pulled away from the open oven. Sadie wasn't timid at all. She rapped two fingers against the shiny crust. A hollow sound echoed back.

"Done," Sadie announced.

Why doesn't Bubbie ever ask me to check the bread? Rebecca wondered. *Bubbie treats me like a little child!* She pushed past her sisters.

"I can do it, too," she said.

"So, give a tap," Bubbie told her. "When dough is done, bread sounds empty."

As Rebecca knocked on the bread with her knuckles, her older brother, Victor, sneaked up and rapped on her head. "Done!" he teased. The twins giggled.

Rebecca tried to swat Victor's arm, but before she could catch him, a rhythmic knock sounded at the kitchen door. Everyone turned to stare as it creaked open. A tall young man wearing a jaunty straw hat and holding a polished cane poked his head into the room.

"Moyshe!" Mama exclaimed.

The man put his finger to his lips, signaling everyone to be quiet, and began sprinkling something in the doorway. Rebecca couldn't see anything in his hand. Her little brother, Benny, squatted down. He looked at the floor, and then up at Moyshe.

"What you are putting on this clean floor?" Bubbie cried.

Moyshe peered into the hallway and looked around nervously. Then he made more frantic sprinkling motions. Finally, he spoke. "It's lion powder," he said solemnly.

Rebecca frowned. "What in the world is that?"

"Why, don't you know?" Moyshe asked. "It keeps the lions away."

Benny's eyes grew wide. "Lions?"

Sadie sniffed. "That's ridiculous. There aren't any lions around here."

"You see how well it works!" Moyshe announced.

Benny heaved a sigh of relief. Sadie and Sophie shook their heads at the silly joke. Rebecca burst out laughing.

Moyshe flashed a gleaming smile. "At least one person in this audience likes my joke," he said. "If you make them laugh, your audience will love you." He winked at Rebecca. "Remember that!"

ᖇᖇᖇᖇ

About the Author

JACQUELINE DEMBAR GREENE
used to read historical novels under an
apple tree in her yard when she was a
girl. She loved to imagine living in a more
exciting time and place. While writing about
Rebecca, Ms. Greene talked with friends
and relatives who recalled their experiences
growing up in the early 1900s. She also
explored New York's Lower East Side and
visited the neighborhoods that would have
been part of Rebecca's world. Ms. Greene
lives in Massachusetts with her husband.
When she isn't writing, she enjoys hiking,
gardening, and traveling to visit
her two grown sons.